HIDE IN LIGHT

James Mann

Mann Or Myth
Atlanta, Georgia

This book would not have been possible without the kind assistance of many people, most notably the lovely LH, June Mann, and my greatest achievement, my son Brian Mann. Special thanks to Sally Fitzgerald and her memories of Flannery that she shared many years ago.

To everyone along the way who helped, this book is for you. And for anyone who didn't help, this book is *about* you.

Photography © Nancy Mullis
Cover: www.MichaelMastro.com

ISBN: 978-0-692-00283-4
Mann Or Myth, Atlanta Georgia
www.mannormyth.com
www.hideinlight.com

Since the original cell split and the first amoeba swam, the world has evolved. The process has continued in million year chunks until the present. At each step, changes are made. Some species adapt to the world by changing their body, defenses, or habitat. If they cannot survive, the process takes them away.

Mankind, with its big brain and doctrines of justice, is no exception. It's just that our timetable is faster, because we are quicker. When we are gone the big rock on which we live will continue to orbit, and perhaps another breed will emerge. Until that day, humans are part of the same process that brought fish onto land, birds into the air. And like the dinosaur, doomed by too much power without sufficient intellect, we too will perish from the earth.

With savages the weak in body or mind are soon eliminated. We civilized men, on the other hand, do our utmost to check the process of elimination...Thus the weak members of civilized society propagate their kind. No one who has attended to the breeding of domestic animals will doubt that this must be highly injurious to the race of men.

Charles Darwin
The Descent of Man (1871)

BEFORE

Sleeping, half in, half out. Cars and trucks roll by and in the quiet room they seem like miles from here. It's dark-thirty; dust hangs in the air like a fog. Adam can hear voices, but he's not sure from where or when. It's the time between dreams and daylight. He understands the words, and tries to place the voices ...

"He passed the damn test three times-we gotta let him go."

"You know he did it. He as much as told us where to look for the body and anyway that machine doesn't know people."

A machine can't find in you what nature never put there. No lies, no doubt, no right or wrong.

Then the old man. "Never work for free. This isn't about hate, not yours. People will find you, call you, hire you to do things they cannot. Don't ask questions to find out why, only how. Walk away if it feels wrong, but if not, do the job. You can do things they only dare." He could see the old man, talking, drinking coffee, looking out the window into the Washington night, almost as if he was back there, in the mist and the rain, waiting to go back to the river with a girl.

That had been the first. A man with a problem, a fear, an anger to dispel, but too weak or too holy to do it himself. He had found the old man by phone and set up a meeting at a lot on the strip. They sat in his car, watching the working girls hustle.

"My daughter is out there, somewhere."

"Doing that?" The old man asked, and the other man nodded, barely, in return.

"Maybe. I don't know for sure. She's been gone six months and I haven't heard from her. Not a sound. The cops took a report, but that was all. I know she is doing drugs, she did at home after her mother left." He stopped, and seemed to lose himself in a memory.

When he spoke again his voice was harder, all traces of the softness he had used before replaced by anger. "I want them gone. This was a nice place, ya know, before that sort of trash came in. Now they line up and down the road, waving their stuff at you when you sit at a light and doing God knows what in cars all around here." He waved his arm around as if to include all they could see. Adam watched the women, brightly dressed, teetering on heels, chewing gum, waiting as the headlights grow big and then fade, or if they were lucky, slow down. The man lit a cigarette and rolled down the window. The smoke drifted out into the cold air and Adam could hear the girls pitch the cars.

"Hey baby, wanna party?"

"You all lonely, sweet thing? Need some company?" If you closed your eyes you couldn't tell where the sound came from, there were so many voices. He opened his eyes and looked out, watched a police car roll slowly by.

"See! They never stop. They just drive by, like they think all these people here are waiting for a bus or something. Why do they do that, just ignore it? What the hell do we have cops for, pay taxes, if they just drive right by it? Fuck."

The man looked shaken, like this was the start of a tirade he had voiced before. Adam knew why they drove by. It wasn't their job. Cops were there for appearances, to comfort the law abiding joe that they were out there, and to remind criminals of what boundaries were left.

Once upon a time, Adam guessed, it had worked. Everyone stayed on his side of the street, did what he needed to do, and left everyone else alone. The cops gave tickets, wrote up reports and kept the peace. The peace wanted to be kept, once. Now it was different. The have-nots are the majority, and they have no rules. It was the beginning of the end, and that was why he had been born.

These people hadn't given up hope. It was more that they had been born without it, without a trace of the humanity once so evident in the world.

It was the children, so far removed from the world the father in the car had lived in that they might as well have been on Mars. These doomed children have been born with all the resources they need to live apart, underneath the world, the same as Adam. They are born to indifference and hate and are reminded, daily, that they are not wanted. No one wants to see them, touch them or think about them. Most people just ignore them, and structure their lives away from them. Their days pass on a tide of boredom and fear. All around are images of violence, physical and psychic, the television that plays nonstop in the corner, the abusive parent. Adam had grown to fear them, admire them, use them. Soon all would be like them, and after them, nothing.

Everyone has hates, fears, things that anger or disgust them. Some people deal with it, bottle it up and go about their lives under wraps, denying to themselves the satisfaction of retribution or redemption. It was the others that had kept Adam in business. The ones who could justify their hate, rage and prejudice into something holy. The holy paid the best, Adam had found, when he would bomb an abortion clinic or kill a AIDS activist for a group who could talk the talk, but needed someone else to walk the walk.

Their children have gone past needing his help. They live on sugar and meth, watching the tinted windows on big cars reflect their pierced nipples and tattoos and they laugh when the car runs a red light to get away from them, just like the news people tell them to. They have hobbies like crack, carjacking and gang bangs. Together, they send out waves of panic and desperation. Alone, they hide below the level of windows, fearful of an errant bullet. What little they had they squandered, and they look around for someone to blame. They need no excuse to hate, to terrorize. It is all they can do, their only glimpse of power.

Some of them, one in a thousand, get out of school with a prayer and run with it. The rest steal, kill and terrorize anything in their path. One in a million, like Adam, would go on to bigger things, if they could meet up with someone like he had, when he met the old man.

He woke up finally, all the way, trying to clear his head. He looked around, placing himself in the room. What city? Why was he here? He saw the envelope on the dresser and the map of Atlanta and remembered the reason. He had traveled far from the first time, with the old man in Washington. The twelve hundred dollars he had gotten then seemed like all the money in the world.

The job had been easy, dumping prostitutes in the Green River. One had looked at the old man and said "Daddy?" the moment before he killed her. When he turned Adam saw what the girl saw, that the old man's face was gone, shrouded now by the features of the man who had hired them. Adam had learned a lot since then. He had perfected over the years the talent he was born with, the ability to change his appearance in an instant, to look like anyone at all. People saw the demon they most feared, every time.

CHAPTER 1

When all you do for hours is drive a van, you have time to examine all aspects of a situation, take things one by one. Adam thought back over all the jobs he had done over the years, from good to bad, and with a few exceptions, he decided that anything that paid the rent, put gas in his van and didn't keep him awake nights was okay. He couldn't say exactly when he realized that he had fallen into this sort of work as a regular thing, to the exclusion of all else, but he knew that his whole life, in little ways here and there had been a sort of training, a process of refinement and hardening that made him stronger than most and colder than anyone he had ever met.

When he was barely more than a child he had realized that he was different from those around him. Instead of scaring him, making him withdrawn, it filled him with a sense of purpose and self-confidence that put most people off. Things that bothered others had no effect on Adam. He could confront the vilest situations with blank-faced indifference, his eyes cold and still, the color of slate, and walk away at the end cash in hand, to the next job.

As a child he had first puzzled and later terrified his mother, a woman who rose in the morning to televised pleas for money and spent the rest of the day arguing with radio talk show hosts. She believed everyone on television, and hated them all. Sitting at the kitchen table with a cup of coffee long cold in her hand and a Marlboro clenched in her teeth, she would rave about the world, its leaders, her neighbors and their kids. No one was exempt, including Adam, who had no brothers or sisters to defend him. The memory of his father had long grown dim, replaced by the denigration thrown up by his mother to his memory, so strong that if Adam closed his eyes he could swear that the back door had just slammed with his father's leaving. His mother rotated targets for her venom, one week the factory that had laid her off, a former friend the next, all accused of anything from theft to adultery, and all without any chance of redemption

She saved as a constant subject an older man who lived across the street, widowed for years, whose solitary joy in life it seemed to Adam was a pair of small white poodles whose leavings always seemed to end up on Adam's front yard. After years of this Adam became sure that his mother could hear the dogs paws touch their grass and would be out of the house bellowing in an instant.

"Hogan, you son of a bitch, I'm gonna call the pound if you don't teach them damn dogs which yard is theirs and which is mine! You hear me, you deaf fool?" She would yell, housecoat wrapped around her like a bullfighter's cape, arms waving in the air, blind to rest of the world, focused.

At the beginning of this behavior when he was younger, he would hide in his room, mortified because his mother was ranting like a lunatic on the front step, and would hope that soon either she would shut up or Mr. Hogan would walk his dogs some other place on earth instead of in front of his house.

After a few years, with the dogs still running loose and his mother running amok, he decided to end it, once and for all, and get some peace. He remembered the bright sun as he walked down the old man's driveway and up his steps. He knew the man was sleeping, as old people do, and wouldn't hear Adam in the house. Once he got to the door he realized that he had no way in and almost turned around and went home until he heard a dog yip inside and he knew that if he didn't end it now it would go on forever. He reached for the doorknob and turned. He felt the tumblers rotate and reach the internal stop. Staring at the door, Adam clinched his arm and turned the knob a little harder until he heard the lock give way, and he was in.

Hogan was lying on a couch, an AARP magazine on his chest, asleep and snoring. The dogs were the same on the floor and Adam tried to remember how old they were and finally gave up, figuring that however old they were they weren't going to get any older. Reaching into his pocket he pulled out a knife taken from his mother's kitchen and sharpened until a human hair would split in two if dropped along the blade. He knelt down next to the animals, listening to the rapid breathing of the pair. Why do animals breath harder when they sleep, he wondered? One of them opened an eye and stared at him, cocking an ear as if waiting for a command. Adam reached over and ran his thumb down the dog's eyelid, and the animal seemed to return to sleep. Bringing his other arm up he slashed the knife across the dog's neck, deep, until it had gone all the way around. Picking up the head and tossing it behind him onto a throw rug he reached for the other animal and did the same. The blade was so sharp that neither dog as much as flinched, and beside them old man Hogan slept, dead to the world. Adam rolled the heads up in the rug and left the house. Walking back home he could hear his mother calling someone on the radio a blow-hard, which was normal. When he got to the house he opened the screen door and entered the kitchen.

"Fixed those dogs for ya. Here you go," he said, dropping the bloody rug on the old, chipped table in the corner. He brushed pass his mother on the way to his room, not hearing the shriek come from her then or later the quiet gasps as she cried, leaning against the stove, staring at the pairs of eyes, stuck looking at a fixed point above her head. He left the house three days later at seventeen, remembering those few days as some of the best he had spent in that place, with his mother silenced and a look of fear in her eyes. He hadn't heard from or about his mother in years, and hadn't been back to the city of his birth since the day he left. He had no time to.

The world was waiting.

CHAPTER 2

Amid the throngs of people in the food court Erin and Kathy inched closer to the Salad Shop and glanced at their watches. "No way in hell we are gonna get lunch and be back to the office by one, I can't make up any time this week, cause I have to pick up Jason everyday. Rob's out of town and I just know I'm not gonna have five minutes to myself," Kathy exclaimed, her face screwed up in frustration, the words pouring out in a rush.

Erin nodded, only half listening, and walked a few steps closer to the girl behind the counter. A man in a suit was ahead, conferring with a pair of guys in overalls with sagging tool belts strapped to their waists. He was getting rather animated, and the pair of workers seemed bored, like they had heard it all a hundred times before.

"Remember, all the lots have to be cleared by Friday or the temporary permit will run out and I will be out hundred grand and you slugs will be out of a job. Have I made myself clear?"

"We gonna eat, or what?" The taller of the men said, as he glanced back at Erin and smiled, his look staying long enough on her that she averted her eyes and stared back at the counter. She had always felt uncomfortable with the more intrusive attentions of men, invaded for a brief moment, and lately, paralyzed for days after. Kathy was still going on about her morning and Erin was glad that she had known her for so long that she could just put herself on auto pilot and nod every few minutes and still feel that she was keeping up her end.

Erin looked around the food court, thinking about the day, her mind coming to rest on what she was going to do about Tyler, her boss.

Every day he found a reason to be in her office, his breath sucking the air out of the room, always standing behind her when she was sitting down at her PC, looking down her blouse. She could see his face reflected in the glass of the pictures on her desk until his face was dimly imaged over the face of her family.

She saw his eyes drop lower and lower until his eyelids were almost shut, and if someone had walked by they would have thought the Troll had fallen asleep standing up. No such luck, as Erin knew. She had made the mistake during one of Tyler's peepshows to turn around in the chair to ask him something and her elbow had nudged him below his belt buckle. She didn't know what was worse, the pressure on her elbow or the grin on his nasty little face when it happened. If he had spoken at that moment Erin knew that she would have exploded, and they could have buried the remains of his rotund body in a shoebox. Luckily he had remained silent, most likely thinking up some new quip to slam her abilities, the kind he managed to slip into almost every meeting they had.

That, Erin decided, was one of the biggest differences between men and women. Men would think nothing of bedding down with an idiot, and in fact some went out of their way, it seemed, to find them. She had always been disappointed by men, from her father up to the present with Ralph, her husband. She had learned over the years to handle most things herself. Over time it had left her feeling drained, tired and gun-shy. When she had spoken to Ralph about Tyler his look of boredom and amusement gave the lie to the words he spoke.

"I'm sorry he's such a pig. Do you want me to talk to him?"

"Why," her voice rising in anger at being spoken to as though she were a child. "It's not you he's hitting on, leering at. I have to work with him, and I have to deal with him."

"Well, if you think you can handle it. I never thought you going back to work was such a great idea, you know. It's not like we need the money, after all," he responded, his mind already miles away.

She thought silently to herself that money was only one of the reasons you went to work. In her case it was because she felt good about what she did, and it gave her an outlet for the energies that the rest of her life couldn't expend. But now, with Tyler practically putting her job on the line every time they spoke she had begun to dread going into the office and facing another day. She couldn't go back to Ralph and tell him that there was nothing she could do. Tyler was buddies with the brothers that had founded the company, and she knew that any action on her part about the situation would only result in her getting fired, or worse, having lip service paid to her needs until she quit.

"Earth to Erin! What time are you getting off work today?" Kathy was asking, with an impatient look to her face.

"I guess around five, if I can finish retyping that report for Tyler."

"Does he ever do anything right the first time, or is this his idea of job security?" Kathy said, and they both laughed. Ahead of them the line had moved up until the man in the suit was waiting to order. Out of the crowd of people next to them Erin could see, or later she thought she saw a short, sloppily dressed man walk up behind the man in the suit and pause for just a moment, not long at all, and walk away. The girl behind the counter kept asking him to order, two or three times before he collapsed. He fell backward, off of Kathy and onto the floor.

Erin thought heart attack, and for a split second wondered about the irony of having heart failure while waiting to eat health food. She stopped wondering as soon as she looked down at the body on the floor. No wonder the guy never made a sound. His head was nearly separated from his shoulders. A line of red started behind one ear and ended up somewhere back in the hairline on the other side. The women stood numb, already in shock, as the man's blood formed a pool around their shoes. Then someone behind them fainted, and broke the silence as they landed.

Suddenly the area, silent a second before, was a riot of noise. Kathy was shaking and crying and looking around either for help or cover and Erin kept hearing a high wailing sound that she finally figured out she was making. Everyone started to move back, staring, until it resembled a crowd at a circus looking in at the center ring. Erin looked but didn't see the two guys who had been with the man before and she could vaguely remember them saying they were going to get chicken instead and leaving the man before he ordered. She was amazed to have recalled that, because it seemed as if it happened about a week ago.

Finally someone in a uniform appeared. His reaction was not one to restore order. He gasped "Shit, this fucker got whacked," and then turned and walked off. He stopped a few feet away and talked into a walkie-talkie.

"Got some guy down here in the food court with his head chopped off ... What? Yeah, he's dead." The man listened to the box for a moment and spoke. "I don't know, he looks as dead as anyone I've ever seen and I ain't gonna touch it for $7.25 a hour, no way. Call whomever you want and get somebody down here, get Dwight or somebody. I'll keep these people down here until the cops come."

The guard moved all the people to one corner of the tables and cleared a path for the paramedics to wheel in a gurney. Erin and Kathy stared blankly as they covered the body and wheeled it away. The puddle of blood on the floor had left Erin feeling faint and numb.

"You ladies see anything? You were standing about a foot behind the man when he went down, right?" Erin's head rose to the voice, coming from a tall man in plain clothes, holding out a badge.

"Sorry, Detective Nelson Banks. I just wanted to see if there was anything you could tell us about what the person was wearing, or how tall he was, you know, like they do on TV?" He smiled, and Erin knew he was just attempting to lighten the moment, but it struck her as somewhat demeaning.

"I don't know much, I mean he was in front of us for just a few seconds it seems like, and then he was gone. He seemed to be a short guy, I guess, with an old gray jacket on and his shirt wasn't tucked in. I don't know if that helps, sorry." As she was speaking, she wondered how she had managed to recall the color of the jacket and then she realized it was because it looked just like the one that Tyler wore everyday.

Kathy was looking over at her without moving her head, and her eyes seemed to grow wider as Erin talked.

"You see anything, lady?" The detective asked Kathy.

"I don't know, I thought I did. I'm not sure."

"How do you mean, you're not sure? Either you did or you didn't. Just try and relate like your friend did." The cop held a gold pen poised over a pad of paper, waiting to write.

"I mean I thought I did until Erin started talking and now I'm just confused. The man I saw was about six-two, six-three and black, with a Bulls jacket on. He was only there for a half-second, you know. I just don't ... " She was cut off from continuing when the cop turned and walked off, toward a group of men and muttering "That's seven." They stood talking amongst themselves, leaving Erin and Kathy alone on the bench. They sat in silence, staring at the yellow tape draped around the place where the body had fallen, the tiles shiny with blood. After a few minutes he came back.

"Sorry to leave you hanging like that. We're having a little trouble with the descriptions we're getting." He was shaking his head as he flipped through the notepad.

"I know we didn't tell you much but isn't it hard to get descriptions when something like this happens?" Kathy asked.

"Most of the time, you'd be right, we don't have enough to go on. Today, you see, that isn't the problem. Seven eyewitnesses. Seven different descriptions of the same occurrence and presumably the same person. Picked a real visible place to knife someone, a food court at noon on a workday." He looked at the women, and shook his head.

"So what's the problem? Do you think he got out of the mall?" Erin asked.

"Yes, I'm sure he did, if he wanted to. See, it's kinda hard to send out a description of an assailant who may be a black man, a short guy with a gray jacket, a redheaded teenager with an earring in his nose or a Puerto Rican man with a baseball cap on. If this don't beat all. Let me take your phone numbers, I'll have you come down to the station if we need more from you."

They drove silently back to the office. Kathy was still shaking, and Erin was lost in thought. She wondered why they had seen two different things. And why did she get a feeling that the person she saw looked a lot like Tyler?

Erin spent the rest of the afternoon in a daze, her eyes seeing red whenever she let them focus on any thing for too long. After a few hours she felt so tired that it was an effort to move, and she knew she had to get home. In all her thirty years she had never seen death, only the aftermath, a box slowly being lowered into the ground holding a person she only dimly remembered. Seeing a life seep across a floor, not fast like running water, but slow enough to watch, felt brutal. Sitting in her car at a traffic light she thought about the people who would grieve the nameless man's passing, the tears and the shock. She wondered if it would be a lot, or would he die alone, in view of many, mourned by no one. She wondered the same about herself.

CHAPTER 3

Like most people he knew he worked here and there, never steady, but always enough and never anything too demanding, either physically or emotionally. The latest one was the sort of thing he could do without even thinking. The situations might vary once in a while, and sometimes he worked for a jerk, but he always got paid. That's all that mattered. When he was in the middle of a job, either sweating half to death or freezing, he never wondered why the job had to be done, what had caused someone to be in a position to hire him, or what was going to happen when he left.

To tell the truth, this one might be ok. The boss was a lady, which never used to happen. Used to be some guy would call him up, tell him when to be where, and that was that. He would show up, get his instructions, do the job and go. Once in awhile he'd get some guy who wanted to chat, which bored Adam no end. He would talk a mile a minute and ask Adam all sorts of stupid questions. Adam asked one guy if he did the same thing to his dry cleaner, did he ask him a million questions? The guy had gotten quiet after that, and looked a little nervous.

But now, this lady, well she was all business. Sharp, classy and calm as hell. Adam wondered if she had ever raised her voice, or if she had ever had a reason to. She had nice legs, but when Adam asked her if she wanted to get a cup of coffee when he was done she looked at him as if he was crazy. He let it go. He always said he never let his job interfere with his real life, and that had gotten him this far, so he guessed he would stick with it.

She had everything ready when he got there-a box, tape and some plastic bags. He picked up the package and slid a bag over the top. It was a huge, thick bag, and if he folded the thing up it would all fit inside. It was heavy as hell though, and his hands kept slipping on the slick surface of the plastic. She handed him a paper towel.

"Be careful it doesn't leak on the floor-I just had them cleaned," she said sharply.

Adam just nodded and started wrapping the end of the bag with tape. She told him to use a lot of it so if the thing moved when he was driving it wouldn't open the bag up. He finished and lifted the package over his shoulder while she opened the lid to the box. He laid the package inside. It landed with a thud, moved, and then lay still. Adam used the rest of the tape to seal the box and then brought some heavy-duty packing tape out from the van, the kind with little bands of steel in it, and wrapped it around the box. It wasn't that he was supposed to ship it anywhere, and most likely nothing would spill out of the box, but Adam wanted to make sure, and anyway it looked good to a boss to see somebody who was motivated, who could add something to a situation.

Adam took pride in his work, if not any interest. He wanted to do a good job, not really for the person paying him, because it wasn't like they would ever need him again, but for himself. Most people only used him once, except for that guy in the Midwest who kept having him excavate stuff and tell him what he found, and that got old real fast. Anyway the guy was weird, always talking about his mother as though she was around the house somewhere, which she wasn't, because no one's mom would let a house look like that one had, or smell like it did. What was that guy's name? Adam wondered. Ed something. Fein, Wynn? Something like that. No, Adam liked the solitary nature of his work. See the people for a little while, do the work, and go home. Maybe watch a movie or read a book. He didn't go out much because he didn't like crowds, and he had long ago quit drinking because most people he met drank to forget things, and Adam didn't have anything to forget. As he was thinking before, one of the good things about his kind of work was the fact that as soon as he finished, he was done. He never took his work home like those lemmings in suits, men and women racing around, having stress heart attacks and raising their kids on the weekends. Adam liked kids but was glad he didn't have any. He liked being able to move around as he pleased, and he didn't think he could explain his job to a kid anyway. He never had to work with a kid, either, but supposed he would if the money was okay.

Speaking of work, he needed to get this one finished. He went back to the van and got his hand truck and rolled the box out the door. He looked around, not really expecting to see anyone, and didn't. The house was pretty swank, and set far enough away from the road that traffic noise never reached inside. Personally, he would go nuts in a place like that, with all the matching sofas and rugs and little knickknacks that looked stupid and cheap, but weren't. He got bored real quick in these places, but then he guessed so did a lot of people, or he'd be out of a job. By the time someone got around to hiring Adam, they always looked bored or nervous, but rarely angry, like you would expect.

"Do you remember what to do next?" the woman said from the front step. "Come back inside when you're done and I'll give you the rest of the stuff."

Adam resisted the impulse to smart off about the remembering part. Just because of the nature of his work people thought he had to be stupid, slow or half crazy. He wasn't any of those things, just a guy doing a job. He knew he was just doing what thousands of others had done before him, in different ways, under different names. He imagined that they all had their reasons, all valid, all unique, (or so they thought). But the reason never changed, not really, not when the result was the same, a solution, a termination, an end. He knew more about the reasons why than those who came before him, which was why he could do what he did, and have it not mean a thing. He knew that in him was the result of all men, and all men will destroy, if given a reason. He was different, distilled. He needed no reason. He did it because it was his nature.

Before him, the intent of evolution had been the adaptation of a species for maximum breeding and survival. He stood at the beginning stages of the process in reverse. Instead of more, he made less. Everyone, given the right circumstances, would need people like him until one day everyone would be as he was.

Because someday no babies will cry, no voices will shout in anger, no tears will spill in horror. Not because the pain will end. Rather, the pain will win. All that is needed is a catalyst.

He walked back to the house and sat down on the couch. She handed him an envelope. It was thick and sort of a creamy white color and inside was some money and a piece of paper. Adam counted the money and stuck the paper in his pocket. The lady had changed into a workout outfit and said she was late for an aerobics class. Adam said sure, he was all done. She walked out with him and he watched as she got into a Lexus and drove away. Adam started the van, and looked into the back at the box. It was still there, wedged against the side, with a heavy blanket over it. He found the blanket handy because sometimes the packages would shift and settle, making just enough noise to interrupt Adam when he listened to the radio. He liked classical music and played it all the time. This always surprised people, maybe they expected him to listen to speed metal, something loud and angry that would hurt your ears. Adam rolled down the driveway and turned onto the street. He made a left and followed the railroad tracks for miles, humming along with Gorecki's *Third Symphony* on the radio and watching the other cars as he passed. He hardly ever saw a cop, and even if he did, he was a good driver so he had nothing to worry about. He thought sometimes he must be almost invisible because he could walk right past somebody with a box like the one in the back, and they never even looked twice. As long as you looked like you knew what you were doing, people left you alone.

He laughed when he remembered taking that rug out of that guy's apartment downtown, and how he thought this was it. He was about halfway to the door before the security guard at the desk called, "Excuse me, sir," and when he turned around he saw he had left a trail of shiny little drops across the gray marble floor. Glancing up at the fat guy at the desk he saw him waving a clipboard.

"You gotta sign out. Building rules, you know."

So Adam leaned the rug against the guy's desk, signed out, and left. Maybe the bag had ripped or something, who knows. But that was the only time he ever got stopped while he was working.

That thing the other day, in the mall, twenty minutes it was done. Walk in, find the guy, slice and walk. He hid in plain sight while the cops talked to the people. They wheeled the body right past him, and one guy told him to wait, they wanted to talk to him, too. He got up and left. He walked slowly around a group of detectives who barely looked up as he walked past. It was over, he was paid, and looking back he couldn't remember what the reason was the man had given him when he hired him. Didn't matter anyway.

He slowed as he saw the empty factories across the tracks. When he turned and went over the rails the van lurched and the package in the back seemed to thump. Adam ignored it and drove on to the end of the road. He stopped between two abandoned warehouses and an old steel plant. He had picked this place because it was miles away from anything and the package could just sit there Adam guessed for months until somebody came across it. Of course he didn't really care what happened to it, and it's not as if anyone ever wanted one of them back anyway. Adam parked and reached under the seat for his bolt cutters. The place had a padlock and a chain through the door that looked about fifty years old. He got out of the van and snapped the rusted metal with one try. He tossed the tool into the van and put the box back on the hand truck. Wheeling it inside he heard rats scurry around, deeper into the deserted building. Adam had heard that rats would eat anything and could chew through wood. He wondered if the packing tape on the box would stop them. Probably not, but what happened after he left wasn't his concern anyway. He rolled the box over into a corner, out of the way of the door. It sat there, quiet and still as he turned around and walked back to the van. Shutting the door to the building he loaded the hand truck and got back in the driver's seat. Gershwin was playing, *Rhapsody in Blue*, and Adam smiled, remembering the lady who played it for him the first time under the hot sky in Utah, when he was taking care of some guy who had been caught selling documents and blackmailing some Mormons. They offered him money and the woman. Adam walked away with the cash and left the woman.

Maybe he would go back there sometime. There was always lots of work between there and L.A., although he hated Los Angeles, with all the gangs and the drive-bys. He hated being on edge all the time, watching his back, fearful of those with even less restraint than he. He looked down the road as he drove until he found a phone booth away from a building and pulled up. He took the paper out and dialed the number on the top. It rang four times and then a woman's voice answered.

"You have reached the Graves' residence. We can't take your call right now so please leave a message."

Adam just stood there, looking at the phone and laughing. He had figured the woman wouldn't be there. Probably got hung up at the gym and forgot the time. Still, he guessed he could just do what she had told him to do anyway, and talk to her the next day when he called about the money. He looked at the paper and started to read. He didn't bother to disguise his voice-what are they gonna do, VoicePrint the entire country? Instead he read the sentences she had given him, to the tape.

" Mrs. Graves. We have your husband. If you want to see him again, do not call the police. We want two million dollars in cash or we will send him back one piece at a time. We will call you tomorrow and tell you where and when."

CHAPTER 4

It was always hot in the squad room, noisy. It just seemed hotter and louder when you were stuck on a case that wouldn't crack, didn't make any sense. Nelson Banks looked over the report for the tenth time in an hour and finally flipped it aside, disgusted.

"Still can't figure the food court guy, can you?" his partner, Phillip Maxwell asked.

"No, and it's starting to nag me, you know? I mean the guy was a grade-A son of a bitch, and you would think you would have to stand in line to kill him, but this mess with the descriptions is nuts. I mean damn, you expect some differences between accounts but seven totally contradictory versions is crazy." He looked dejected, and got up to pour another cup of coffee, grimacing as he drank.

"Go over it again. Maybe something will jump out if you tell it enough," Maxwell asked, grabbing a legal pad and a pen.

"All right, from the top. Deceased was John Portelli, 46, founder and sole owner of Portelli Construction. He was divorced three times; two kids, and from all accounts heading for split number four when he was killed. Made his money, which was a lot, from being in the right place at the right time and getting government contracts for new hospitals, jails, you name it. Always seemed to be either the low bidder, or the only one, and even when nobody else would touch a job, like that landfill out near the old water reservoir that raised such a stink from the neighborhood groups? He was set to begin construction on it next week, and was about to finish clearing off the land the Friday before he was killed."

"He was running behind on that, I hear?"

"Yeah, he was in and out of court with some of the locals because they said he was going to ruin one of the oldest parts of the city. Seems that after the water plant shut down nature took over and the old holding ponds and whatnot grew into a sort of wildlife sanctuary. Some of it had trails and stuff going through, people had picnics there, whatever. It was a nice place, went there once a few years back. From what I understand he leveled the place, without a twig or a stick left. I think what really got the people going was when it came out that he was going to lose money on the whole deal."

"Well it only looks like he's gonna lose, right? I mean, you don't get as fat as Portelli by giving shit away, so there was something else going down." Phillip was writing on the pad, his feet up on the desk.

"Rumor has it he was in line to build a five acre jail down south and the state would look at him a little better if he helped them out on this. Sure got some folks riled up. A lot of them weren't real happy about it."

"Unhappy enough to kill him?"

"I don't think so. I mean, what's the point? The contracts are signed, the land is cleared. The company is going to finish the job, no matter what, so if the intent in knocking him off was to stop it then somebody wasted their time." Nelson rubbed his eyes and stood up from the desk and paced around.

"How about the wife? Think she could have been fed up enough to want him gone? I mean, the fact that he fooled around wasn't exactly a secret."

"No kidding. But of course she would know that, seeing as how that is how he met her. I guess there could be something to it, because surviving him would leave her with a lot bigger chunk of change than just leaving him, but I don't think she's the type to have something like this done, and we know that she didn't do it herself."

Maxwell laughed a bit and said, "Yeah, at least all the descriptions were of men. I'd quit and take early retirement if somebody had said they saw a lady that day. Shit! Can you imagine the press we would get if that got to the papers? We already look foolish not being able to get a description of a man who walked into the most crowded mall in Atlanta at noon and killed a man in front of a courtyard full of witnesses."

Around them the room was alive with people. Hookers smoked and swore under the fluorescent lights, and in a corner, away from the main room, drunks lay on the benches and floors of the holding cell, either asleep or still high from the night before. Every so often one would bellow out at the guard at a desk in front of them who would ignore it. Sitting at a desk where two kids about seventeen handcuffed to a bar. The smaller one spoke, his face quivering like he was on the verge of tears.

"You gotta let me go to the bathroom! I mean, this isn't funny anymore!"

His friend, spike-haired, the silver earring in his nose the only bright spot about him, nudged him quiet with an elbow and spoke sharply.

"The man don't have to do shit. Just shut up and pipe down. This will take twice as long, you keep running your mouth."

The cop at the desk looked up from his computer and stared at the smaller boy.

"Your friend here is right. He's been here before, knows how it goes. Just shut up and answer my questions and soon enough you'll get to go into a nice room like the one over there, and see, it has a toilet that you can use." He motioned over to a cell against the far wall. It was about the size of a closet and already had three large men in it, who were staring out at the teenagers through the bars, and could overhear the conversation at the desk.

"Yeah buddy, we got a place for ya! Little man need to go pee-pee?" The cell erupted in a riot of noise, and as the man spoke to him the younger boy felt his pants get warm all of a sudden, and when the sound of liquid hitting the floor became louder his cuff mate began kicking at his chair, trying to get away from him.

"Dammit, you little homo! Ain't no way I'm getting in there with you! I told you to stay at home, didn't I? Now you go and piss all over the floor. Damn."

Banks walked over and looked down at the PC screen. "Got some rock hounds here, Marris? How much they have when you picked them up?"

"The little one was heavy, about fifteen vials worth. The other one, he just was standing around, all innocent, to hear him tell it. Except for the gun that we found in his underwear when we patted him down, that is."

"You guys figure on making a little money, sell some rock, have a big weekend?" Nelson spoke right down in the young one's face, then stared for a while. He could feel the fear come off the boy, almost a scent. Out of the corner of his eye he glanced at the other one. He seemed unmovable, sullen. He continued speaking to the smaller one.

"See those guys over there, in that cell? Know why they are there? See the one with the tattoos, the friendly one who was talking to ya before?" The frightened boy nodded. "Seems he works the same sort of business you two go-getters were trying. Small world, huh? I think you guys will have a nice time comparing trade secrets, especially since where you guys got busted is smack in the middle of his turf. Don't know if he'll like that too much, whatcha think? You done with these guys, Marris?" The man nodded and said sure, uncuffing the pair from the desk.

"Come on, let's get you in the hole." Banks reached down to the larger one and picked him up, leading him to the cell. He was trying to keep his hands as far away from the hands of his cuff mate, who was whimpering as he shuffled to the cell.

"This is bullshit, man. I got a permit for that gun. Check it out." It took everything Nelson had not to reach up and rip the earring out of the punk's nose.

"You ain't got no gun permit at seventeen, smart guy. So unless you want to tell me where you got it, I don't want to hear you breathe, understand?" The boy wisely stayed silent, letting himself be led.

They were almost to the cell door when he turned to face Banks.

"Got something you might want to know, if you take me somewhere other than in there with them." He looked confident, almost cocky.

"I doubt seriously that anything that comes out of your mouth is of much interest to me, frankly. You're just trying to narc out some friends and walk. I don't do that shit, not with little guys like you."

"Nah, it ain't like that. This dude wasn't a friend of mine. Just some guy I saw at the mall, you know, the day that guy got slit?" He had Bank's attention now, and the detective pointed to a chair and told him to sit. He locked the smaller boy up and pulled a chair up next to the waiting teenager.

"What's your name?" he asked.

"Robert Morris. You gonna let me out of these handcuffs? They're starting to hurt my wrists."

"Maybe in a minute if you tell me anything interesting. For right now I'll leave them on, maybe they'll make you talk faster. Now what do you know about the thing at the mall? You in on it, maybe?"

The boy sat up in the chair. "Hell no, I don't do nothing like that! I just saw somebody, understand?"

"Who did you see? We got a lot of people who saw the guy leave the food court." He didn't bother to mention that the information they gave had so far been of no help.

"Any of them follow the dude into a bathroom and watch him drop something in a trash can then walk out and get in a van?"

CHAPTER 5

Banks moved the boy into a questioning room. He brought in a tape recorder and a sketch artist, in case Morris said anything.

"So tell me again why you followed this guy. I mean, he just killed somebody. Me, I'd walk the other way."

"I didn't really follow him, it's just that I was going into the hallway where the bathrooms are and he was in front of me, see? I went into the men's room and there he was, washing his hands. He looked up at me in the mirror and I walked past him to a stall and did my business."

"Then what?" Banks was ready for this kid to say something worthwhile.

"Well, I went to leave, cause I didn't think I should hang around the guy, probably not the type to have strangers staring at him, ya know? As I was leaving I saw him drop a knife in the trashcan. I got scared and hustled out the door. It didn't look like he even noticed me, I don't think, but I wasn't taking any chances. But it was kinda like he didn't care if I did see him- it was weird. I left the bathroom and walked out of the mall, and when I was in the parking lot I saw him again, getting into a white van and driving off. That's all I know, I swear. You gonna let me go on this gun thing now?"

"Hold on, one thing at a time. What was the guy wearing?"

"I think it was just blue jeans and a T-shirt. He had a coat on, like a windbreaker. Red."

"What color was his hair? You catch that, maybe?" Nelson wasn't convinced that this kid had seen something. Most people in the boy's position would talk a blue streak if they thought it might buy them a break. Still, you had to check it out and with the investigation sitting dead in the water, anything that might be a lead had to be run up the flagpole. You never know.

"Oh yeah, his hair was black. Real black, like Elvis' used to be? I mean, it almost looked like Indian hair, black and straight. It wasn't very long, I don't think."

"Anything else about how he was dressed? What kind of shoes, any marks on him, like a tattoo or a scar?"

"No, I don't remember anything like that. I never looked at his feet, so I couldn't tell ya about the shoes, and I don't remember seeing any tats. The dude wasn't real eye-catching, to tell the truth. I mean, if I saw him out in a crowd I wouldn't be able to pick him out again for nothing."

"So why now? What made you remember him when you did see him?"

"Damn, I saw what happened, I was walking right by there when that chick fainted and the people started yelling and stuff. I just thought I should get the hell out of there until it got a little quieter, you know?"

"Why didn't you talk to one of the detectives? You understand that leaving the scene of a crime is against the law? Are you just one of those no snitch types, or did you have a reason to avoid the cops?" Nelson figured it was the latter, and this kid didn't seem like the type, carrying or not, to provoke a confrontation with police. Not many kids were these days. Used to be, when he was growing up, you trusted the cops, felt safer when they were around.

It was one of the reasons he became a cop, he guessed, to try and provide that feeling of security to people, protection. He had kept that feeling with him for about two weeks on the street. The first time he answered a domestic call he got the shit beat out of him by both the man and the woman (who had called the cops in the first place), and then she wouldn't press charges when they got there, even though her lips were cracked and bleeding and her eye was rapidly turning black. When he tried to change her mind, she started slapping him hard against his ear and he was so stunned for a moment that the large, drunk man in the corner, who had tired of beating on his wife and was taking a rest, had snuck up behind him and was ready to brain him with the butt end of a pistol. If Nelson's partner hadn't slammed the guy in the knees with a nightstick Banks might be dead now. No, things had changed, a lot, and every day he found another reason to give it up, stop beating himself up about it and just retire and go into private security like some of his old coworkers. That's where the money was, playing to people's worst fears and paranoia by creating armed camps for them to live and work in, surrounded by fences and guards with dogs and Uzis. It wasn't real exciting, but maybe he had lived an exciting life too long.

The boy in the chair was fidgeting around, and Nelson had to ask him again why he didn't come around earlier.

"Were you holding, going to a buy at the mall?" He looked down at the inventory sheet attached to the kid's arrest record, looking for a beeper. Yep, there it was.

"Nah, not that day. I was going to get some new Fila's, you know, shoes? I just didn't want to talk to no man about some shit I didn't really see all that well, right? So you gonna let me walk on this gun thing, didn't I help you out?"

Nelson was about to answer, tell the kid no, when someone knocked on the door to the room.

"Come on," he answered. The door opened and a uniformed cop came in.

"Maxwell wants to see you, says he has something you might want to see."

"Tell him I've seen it before, it wasn't that interesting." Both men laughed for while, and the kid joined in. The two cops both turned to him at the same time and told him to shut up.

"I'll be over in a minute, after I finish with this guy."

"Sure, I'll tell him." The uniform left and Banks returned to the kid.

"Tell me about the van. White, anything else? Old, new, windows, what?"

"Nothing special, just a white van. Didn't have any windows. Had Georgia plates, though."

"Any chance you read the tag, can tell me what it was?"

"No, the guy pulled off pretty quick. I couldn't see anything."

"All right, if you don't have anything else I'm gonna take you back and run priors on you. If they come up clean, and this information turns out to be any help, then maybe we can talk about you leaving us. Until then, you stay with your buddy and his friends in the tank."

"That little guy most probably dead by now, don't ya think?" the kid said, smirking a little bit.

"Either that or engaged. Let's go." He led the boy out and handed him back to Marris, and left the area. He found his partner at his desk, looking over a fax.

"What ya got?"

Maxwell read a few seconds longer and looked up.

"Remember Clarence Williams, was around here until '87, '88?"

"Yeah, good cop. He went to Florida, right?" Nelson asked.

"Right, around Jacksonville. Working homicide down there. I was on the phone with him a while ago, and happened to mention this food court thing to him. Seems he had something like that a few years ago."

"People getting beheaded for lunch down there too?"

"No, it was the description thing, like we got. Seems somebody went into a women's dorm at the university one night and beat the living shit out of three nursing students. Killed two of them and almost wasted the third, but she passed out and I guess the guy figured he was done. Anyway, when they started talking to the other girls in the dorm they got a lot of them who had seen the guy, I mean at two in the morning the only people you see in a dorm are supposed to be girls or security guards."

"Or boyfriends, sneaking out."

"Yeah, of course, but they all checked out. No, the weird thing was, Williams said, was that all the descriptions were different. Way different."

"They caught the guy, right? Some local who had been in and out of mental hospitals for most of his life, if I remember."

"They arrested him, but he never went to trial. Seems he had an alibi they couldn't shake, plus he didn't have a motive, not one that you could get up in front of jury with." Maxwell looked back down at the paper in front of him and read some more.

"So, what are the descriptions like. Match anything we got?"

"Hell no, it's just that it seems sorta unlikely that the fifteen people they talked to that night all saw somebody different. I don't know, might be nothing. Just thought you might want to know that maybe we got something going here." Maxwell handed him the fax.

"Say anything in here about a white van at the scene?"

"Yeah, how did you know that?"

Nelson smiled for the first time in a week.

CHAPTER 6

Erin didn't go to bars as a rule, and wouldn't have when Kathy asked this time except that Ralph was away on business and she didn't want to go home, watch T.V and stare at the walls. Since the killing she found it hard to sleep and when she did finally drop off, she had dreams of someone who looked like Tyler chasing her around and around a large room with only one door. No matter how she moved, or how fast she ran (and since he was about fifty pounds overweight she always thought she could outrun him, if need be) he always was one step ahead of her, grinning and grabbing for her. She could never reach the door marked "EXIT".

So when Kathy suggested getting a beer after work, Erin said sure. Maybe listening to someone else's problems would let her forget hers, for a while. They went to a restaurant near the office and even though it was early, they couldn't find a table. They sat at the end of the bar away from the crowd and ordered drinks.

Kathy was the first to speak.

"Has that detective called you? I talked to him the other night and it doesn't sound like they have made any progress."

"Yeah, I went down there a few days ago. He was telling me that something similar happened in Florida a couple of years ago, at least they think it may be connected. Kinda makes you feel strange, doesn't it? I mean, someone gets killed right in front of you and you can't really do anything to help. I've never been involved in anything like this before, have you?"

Kathy waited a moment before answering, and Erin felt that perhaps she had asked the wrong question. Kathy was always so chatty, so outgoing and loud. Even though they worked together Erin really didn't know that much about her friend, other than she was originally from Jackson, Mississippi and had been married once. She sat while Kathy was silent, picking at the napkin under her drink. Finally she spoke.

"I haven't told this to anyone since I moved here, and I don't know why I'm telling you, but what the hell. I got raped a few years ago, at Christmas." She spoke quickly and then looked away.

"Oh God, I'm sorry! I didn't mean to bring it up. What happened?"

"It was before I moved here, in fact it was why I moved here. I was coming out of a department store a few days before Christmas and it was dark, and I was parked under the only lamp without a bulb in the whole fucking lot and some guy came out and grabbed me after I had unlocked the door. He pushed me into the backseat and held his hand over my mouth. I lay in the car for about three hours before I could move enough to get out. And you know the weird thing?"

"What?"

"The guy at the mall looked just like him. I know its nuts, but when I saw him out of the corner of my eye I was sure. Same face, same coat, everything. I mean, isn't that weird? That's why I freaked when you started talking to Banks, and giving your description. I thought we would have seen the same thing, but when you started talking I just thought I had gone crazy! I mean, what would cause something like that?"

Erin didn't know. All she could remember was that until the detective had spoken to her, asked her some questions, she couldn't remember a thing about the man. It was only once she started talking that the image of the short fat man in a gray jacket came to her. Since then she had wondered with an uneasy feeling what had forced the picture of Tyler into her mind. She couldn't say for sure if the man had really looked like that, but somewhere in her something said he was the one.

Kathy rose and excused herself to go to the bathroom. Erin glanced at her watch and decided that it was about time to go, although she didn't know why. With Ralph out of town there wasn't any great rush to get home. She picked up a menu off the bar and thought about ordering. She was absorbed in it, enough that she didn't hear the stool next to her slide away from the bar and a person sit down.

"Can you recommend anything to eat?"

She jumped. "Ah, what? I'm sorry, I guess I just started daydreaming or something." Erin was startled, and a little uncomfortable. She never liked meeting people in places like this, and she tried not to get started in a conversation if she could help it.

"I was just wondering if the food was any good. Have you ever been here before?" The man asked, and as Erin shook her head no she looked at him, trying to place where she had met him before. She had the oddest feeling that she had encountered him somewhere. Maybe it was the hair, shiny black and straight to his shoulders. You wouldn't forget hair like that.

"Hey, I gotta run." Kathy returned to the bar and picked up her beer and finished it in a gulp.

"Why, what's the matter?" Erin didn't want her to go and leave her alone at the bar, not with this person next to her. She could leave as well, but she didn't really want to go home and she was getting hungry. Kathy was rummaging through her purse, which was as messy as her office and her house.

"Oh, I called home to talk to Rob and he has some clients coming over and needs me to help. Here, found my wallet. How much is it?"

"Oh, don't worry about it, you get lunch next week."

"I hope it turns out better than the last time!" Kathy said with a snort, and yelled back "Call me later" over her shoulder as she left the bar.

"Bad time?" The man beside her asked, and Erin looked at him strangely.

"Yes, you could say so. We were at the mall when the man was killed at the food court, right in front of us."

"That must have been horrible. I didn't hear about it. It happened at a mall? I guess they caught the guy, right?" The man rested his head on his hand and took a drink from a glass of clear liquid.

Who couldn't have heard about it? It was all over T.V for a week, and the editorials in the paper had picked it up as a statement for all that was wrong with society in general. The more Erin learned of the man who had been killed she saw that it wasn't just a random, hit-or-miss type of event. The man had stirred up a lot of folks, and it was rumored that he was shady, business wise. Still, she couldn't imagine a bunch of tree-huggers getting pissed off enough to kill somebody. Where had this guy been that he missed it?

"Makes you wonder, doesn't it? I mean, a man standing there getting lunch and bam! he's dead. I guess it beats cancer, or something like that. Wonder what he did, to get somebody worked up enough to kill him?" the man asked, and Erin was surprised that their thoughts were running along the same track.

"I don't know. I was just thinking that myself." She felt somehow that they were on the same wavelength, connected. They talked for a few minutes and he asked if she had chosen something to eat yet.

"I guess I'll just go on home and fix something there."

"Oh, now don't say that. I was thinking of ordering some nachos or something, why don't you stay and share them with me? I won't bite, I promise." He paused and looked at her, and then went on. "See, I'm in town for business and this place was across the street from my hotel and I just wandered over. I don't like to eat alone."

"What kind of work do you do? " Erin couldn't believe she was chatting with a perfect stranger in a bar. Had things gotten that bad at home? Yeah, maybe they had.

The man sat quietly for a moment before he answered, finding the right words.

"I travel around the country for different folks who need things done, troubleshooting, stuff like that. Not very exciting, I'm afraid."

Erin laughed, and said "Sort of a hired gun, right?"

The man froze and his eyes locked in on hers. He stared for a moment and Erin felt a flash of something run through her, not a sexual feeling, more like a sort of deja vu. The feeling that she knew this man from somewhere was stronger than before. Where?

"Yeah, I guess you could say that, sometimes."

They ordered some food and talked. She found herself telling him things she hadn't spoken even to her husband. Not that he would care, particularly. Maybe that she knew she would never see this guy again made it easier to talk, freer. She told him about her job, and Tyler.

"So what's this guy like? Sounds like a real slug."

"That's exactly it! He's a slug! He's a hairy little troll, with breath like truck exhaust." They both laughed.

"He's always hovering around me, trying to peek down my blouse or at my legs. I was going up the steps the other day and when I got to the top I looked back and he was down there, staring up my skirt." She shuddered. "I almost got sick. God, I hate that man!" She caught the bartender's eye and ordered another beer.

"Do you like your job? I mean, why do you take it? Why don't you go somewhere else? " He looked at Erin, concerned.

"I don't know, I mean my husband earns enough that I don't need to work. It's just that I can't run and be a quitter. I wouldn't be able to face myself. I think it would make me feel like a easy mark, you know, if something ever happened again." She thought about Kathy, and her experience in a parking lot. Did she ever feel like a target? She felt bad that she hadn't known, but Kathy wasn't the type to show that much of herself, didn't talk much about her past. Maybe that was why. Erin felt like Tyler was forcing himself on her, in a long, slow, drawn out method of rape. Would it be easier if it happened in an instant, in a dark parking lot with no one around? She didn't know. The pressure of the situation was killing her. Everyday that she let it go on was like she was agreeing to it. She wished she could stop him, make him suffer, like he had her, in a way that he would remember and carry with him for the rest of his life. She had pondered all the options, and none of them were good. She could quit, and he would go on with someone new, oblivious to the pain he dealt. Or she could sue him, but that would be a matter of convincing total strangers of what happened, and she didn't know if she had it in her to do that, and most likely it wouldn't work anyway.

"So tell me about your job. Who do you work for?" Erin tried to make small talk.

"I don't work for any one company or person. It isn't that sort of thing." He could tell she was lost, confused.

"What I mean is that I have a service and when somebody needs it, they call me. I don't always know how they find me, but if they can pay then usually I'm game. It's just a job, same as any other." He ate a few chips off the plate between them. Erin thought he looked strong, with a good build. His hands were long, clean. She got the feeling that he didn't do a lot of outdoor work, but that he had a great power. He seemed smart enough, but not in a show off way.

"Do you travel a lot? What brought you to Atlanta?" Erin liked talking to him, even though she felt like she was somehow breaking a rule.

"Some folks had a problem so they called me in. I took care of it in a day and I'm just waiting to see where I go next before I roll out of here. Maybe further south, down to Miami. This is strange, here we are sharing food and I haven't learned your name. Mine's Adam Winter. What's yours?"

"Erin Welch. Nice to meet you. Listen, I have to be going."

She gathered her things and started to pull a credit card out of her wallet. Adam picked up the check and told her it was on him.

"Have to use the expense account or they take it away! It was nice meeting you. I hope everything works out with your boss. If you feel like talking about it, or need some help, let me know." He handed her a card and without looking at it she dropped it into her purse.

"Thanks. I hope you get another job soon. Miami would be nice, if you can keep from getting robbed, I guess. Never been there, myself. Well, thanks again for dinner." He shook her hand and she left, wanting to call Kathy as soon as she got home. She felt compelled to talk to her about what had happened, and to see if there was anything she could do. At the door she turned and looked back, to see if she had forgotten anything. The area where they had been sitting was now empty. Where had he gone, so quickly? It was odd, but she had better things to wonder about as she got to her car and drove home.

Erin liked her neighborhood, in the suburb of Atlanta called Decatur. She was close to town, and her area hadn't yet been victimized as much as some others by the crime that seemed to flow out of the city. She had friends, people she had lived near for years, who had been robbed or attacked and had surrendered to it and moved, out away from the city to the more rural areas. They felt safer there, and believed the problem to be a matter of location, which she knew it wasn't. It was just that the closer to the city you got, the faster things seemed to decay. She knew it would reach her and them soon enough. Her friends voted every time for bonds to build more jails, and against public transportation, and had great parties when the Republicans took over Congress, with their promises to wipe out welfare and clean up government, as if that would make a difference. She guessed they thought if someone had to ride a bus to come to work, or needed a handout now and again that maybe they didn't want them around after all. None of them could be called racist, or prejudiced, not in the traditional way. But they all looked at Erin and rolled their eyes, and cut out newspaper stories about the latest drive-by or fast food hold-up, convinced that she was living in a snake pit that they had escaped.

Still, she liked it here, and she couldn't imagine herself living so far away from the things she enjoyed, like the High Museum or Little Five Points. Until the attack at the mall, crime had been an abstract notion to her. Now she had seen it, been a part of it. She wondered what could cause something like that to happen, and decided that some people just felt no other way out, and struck back in violent ways.

She pulled into her driveway and parked under the pecan tree next to the house. No sign of Ralph's car, so she guessed that he wasn't able to leave his meetings early and fly home. Somehow this notion didn't bother her too much. It wasn't like they connected any more. She remembered hearing a song one time, "What do you do when it quits being new?" She had thought it funny at the time, but now she understood it and it wasn't as cute as she had thought.

She kicked off her shoes and checked the answering machine. No calls, which was good. She felt a slight pounding in her head, the start of a headache. It had been a while since she had drunk anything, so maybe the two beers she had at that bar didn't react well with her. Maybe she should lie down and watch some T.V or something. It was only seven o'clock, too early to go to bed.

When she woke up, she was dazed. It was dark outside and Erin couldn't remember dozing off. Her neck hurt from sleeping on the couch and she blinked to try and clear her eyes. Finally she heard the phone ringing. She reached for it, trying to right herself on the couch.

"Hello?"

"Where have you been? I've been calling for three hours and kept getting your machine." It was Tyler.

"If you got the machine why didn't you leave a message? And why are you calling me at home?" She was wide-awake now. The notion of him calling her here and invading her private life made her blood boil.

"I didn't want to leave a message. Didn't want your husband to get jealous, you know." Even his voice was slimy, she thought.

"I don't see why my husband would care if my boss called me about work. This is about work, isn't it? Because if not, I'm tired and I need to get to bed."

"Calm down. Geez, you are always so testy. You need to lighten up, be a little friendlier. Never know what it might do for you, if you don't try it, am I right?"

Erin didn't miss the implication, and resisted the impulse to curse at him.

"What do you want that can't wait till tomorrow?" Erin spoke slowly, trying to calm herself.

"Just wanted to know if you are ready for the presentation tomorrow. Got all the reports finished, shit like that?" He was using what Erin called his "stern father" voice, the one that made her feel like an errant six-year-old.

"Yes, I did. I told you that before I left today, remember? I have the reports and charts in the conference room, reserved for nine. Is there anything else?" She desperately wanted off the phone.

"Yeah, make sure you wear that white dress of yours, you know the one?" he said with what could have been a chuckle, but Erin didn't hear it. She had a hard time understanding what he was saying. Why did he care what she wore? It wasn't like she was giving the meeting, he was. All she would do, like always, was pass out the materials and generally look like a secretary, which wasn't her job at all.

"What did you say?"

"Just wear that sexy white thing. I like it."

"What are you talking about? What difference does it make what I wear?"

"None really, I mean I just like the way it looks on you, that's all." He sounded almost human, and maybe she had overreacted.

"Sorry, it just sounded strange. Thank you for the compliment."

"You bet, just wanted to make sure. I mean, when you wear that thing and walk in front of a window, a guy can see right through it, and man, you are stacked."

Erin dropped the phone, and couldn't hear the sound of Tyler on the other end, or the dial tone after he hung up. All she heard was a sound like a swarm of wasps in her head, and she was shaking, and felt like crying.

She walked upstairs and flung open her closet, tossing clothes around until she found the dress. She ripped it off the hanger and tore into it, possessed. Buttons flew in all directions and she could feel her fingernails snag in the expensive fabric. In minutes the dress was a pile of rags at her feet, and she was panting, covered in sweat. She went into the bathroom and turned both knobs on the shower all the way up, until the room was fog shrouded. She stepped into the water fully clothed. Her dress quickly plastered itself to her as she gasped for breath, the fabric molding itself to her legs as the water washed over her while she sobbed, her stomach rolling at the image of herself in his eyes with no face, just her form.

CHAPTER 7

Adam disinterestedly watched the hotel television set, and closed his eyes from time to time, waiting. Most of his life was spent waiting. Sometimes, like the present, he wasn't totally sure of what he was waiting for. Information, employment, he didn't know. He flipped from station to station, trying to find something that would hold his attention. One had a ball game, the Braves pounding someone, another had a movie. Finally he found a station with the news, and left it there.

The woman on the screen was going on about a rally in Florida. He watched the set as crowds of people with blue signs marched back and forth in front of an office building, matched on the other side of the street by earnest looking people with handwritten placards filled with bible verses and angry slogans. He guessed it was an abortion clinic, and when he watched a few moments more he found he was right.

The place and the situation looked like the one he had been at a few years ago in Texas. He had bombed a doctor's office one night, on the eve of the Republican convention. He remembered that he had wanted to go ahead and do it during the day, explaining that it was just as easy to him, he wouldn't get caught either way. He didn't think they would go for it, and he was right. The five men in string ties and red, scared faces said no, they didn't want to hurt anyone, just close the place down. They had tried to find out Adam's brand of faith, and couldn't, mainly because he didn't have any. They had tried to close down the clinic, but hadn't done that either. If they had done it his way, they would have. He tried to tell them that you would have to blow up ten buildings to achieve what the killing of just one of the patients or doctors inside would bring. They hadn't listened.

Now the guy in Florida, the longhaired one, David, he had been there in Texas and had obviously taken the words to heart. He had been arrested a while ago for shooting a doctor at one of the clinics. Adam smiled as he thought about it. A few more people like that and he would be out of a job.

All around him he could tell that the world was such a different place than it was when he was younger and just beginning to realize his path in life. He didn't work as much as he once had, and it wasn't because the world was becoming a calmer place. No, it fact it was 180 degrees the other way. On the street he recognized more and more of his kind, with blank, sullen looks that gave off an aura of rage, and a fearlessness that came with the acceptance of having nothing to live for.

Adam blamed it in on the television, CNN, things like that. It had made the world a much smaller, less mysterious place. When he was a kid and something happened in another part of the world, or the other side of the country, you found out about it the next morning in the paper. By then the emotion that it could cause had dissipated, and in its place were editorials and endless analysis, all of which blunted the impact of the deed. Now all you had to do was turn on the T.V at any hour, any day, and there was a killing, a war, something happening half a world away. You saw it live, and felt forced to have a reaction, to make it a part of your life.

He remembered being in Detroit when the Rodney King verdicts came down. The city had become a police state, the streets and shops as empty as during a bomb scare. He had been in a poolroom at the time and remembered watching the local black leaders mouthing on and on about how shamed they felt, and how they had demanded that the city of Detroit do something or they would march. There had been a suggestion, actually a promise, of a riot and the leaders laid it all at the hands of the police and mayor. He recalled thinking that the actions of a jury in California had nothing at all to do with the conditions of inner-city residents of one of the most violent places on earth, but he hadn't voiced it out loud. That was one of the few cities in which he felt uncomfortable and scared.

He had defended himself far beyond what anyone would guess by looking at him, but cities like Detroit, New York, Miami and parts of the south were places he would hesitate to enter because they were so far along in the process of destruction, four and five generations, that the odds of a random, senseless attack were greater.

Everybody wants power. Some only needed a little bit, and got it at work, with their kids or in a hundred small ways. Others, like the teens he had been with here in Atlanta, or the gangs of South Central L.A., saw power only in killing someone else, for no reason at all. Much like a deer hunter who kills for sport and leaves the body in the woods, they cruised neighborhood streets and back alleys and fired at whatever moved. Sometimes he felt old, out of step, like he was working in a small corner of a canvas while those younger than him were painting the Sistine Chapel.

He thought about the woman at the bar. He didn't have another job lined up, or he would have gotten in his van and left town the same day as the knifing at the mall. Instead he lingered around Atlanta, watching the city spin around him, festooned with banners, signs and bumper stickers all announcing the coming of the Olympics in a few months.

He had been at the games once, in 1972. He hadn't seen a moment of competition. Instead he spent the entire two weeks in a hotel room wearing a ski mask and pointing a rifle at some athletes from Israel while the world sat glued to the T.V. When the killing was over he had argued with the man who had hired him over his money. The discussion lasted too long, and he killed the Arab. It was the only time he had ever killed for reasons of his own. He did it to make a statement, set an example. It must have worked because he has been paid on time ever since. He walked out of the hotel room dressed as an Interpol officer, and no one had stopped him. Munich was cold and he felt at home there in spite of the fact that Germany had tried for decades to make the world forget the deeds of people like him.

Their only fault was being too vocal, too vain. He could point to a dozen spots around the world where the seeds of even greater destruction had taken root and would flourish all because the people in charge didn't want the limelight as much as they wanted to win. He knew that in the near future entire nations of people would cease to exist on the Earth, much like the passenger pigeons in America.

It was once the most populous bird in the country, and now it was gone, hunted and poisoned out of existence. He knew first hand that in places like Africa, Central America, here in downtown America or on the reservations in the west, people were being starved, shot and drugged to death everyday, by others who would rather command a desert or an empty city than a people.

So he had hung around Atlanta, and let his body rest. The woman at the bar had been easy to follow. He had watched them go to a car about an hour after the attack and followed the route they took back to the office park where they worked. It was just a matter of time before he ran into her again. He didn't really think anything would come of it, but he wanted to get her talking about the killing, see if she could describe him. From what he could tell when they spoke she couldn't.

None of them ever could. Her worry about her boss, some asshole named Tyler, seemed to cause her more concern than witnessing a murder. That's why he had given her his number. She didn't seem the type to want anything done, but you never knew.

He flipped around the television one more time, and paused for a moment on a cable horror movie, big on fake blood and body parts. Most of these were laughable, made by people who only guessed at what they portrayed. But recently he had seen a movie,

Nek, something from Europe, with seven ritual suicides enacted. Some were so real he could tell from the eyes of the dying that it was not acting, but a new version of the old snuff movies like those he had once helped create. The movies he had made, in dirty abandoned warehouses in New York, had been sold by word of mouth to aberrant collectors, people with money and strange tastes. So when he had seen the recent tapes, for rent in a video store near the mall where he had knifed the man, he was amazed. He felt old, outdated.

CHAPTER 8

Erin heard things in the dark midnight that normally she slept through. A clock ticked, the refrigerator cycled on and off. How many things went on in the world that she hadn't experienced? She had seen one at the mall that day, and still another listening to Tyler. She could hear the incessant buzzing of the phone, off the hook downstairs. The sound seemed vast and alive, as she crouched huddled in the corner. Her wet clothes left a smear of moisture on the wallpaper behind her body. She had no idea how long she had been there, in the ebony stillness of her bedroom. She remembered leaving the shower when the spray ran cold, draining the water heater. Her teeth chattered so fiercely she feared she would bite her tongue.

Slowly, feeling her way up the wall with numbed hands, she stood. Water dripped in a pattern on the carpet. Her feet felt the dampness of it between her toes, and she remembered the stain of blood slowly moving across the tile floor of the food court. Her fingers moved to take off the dress, but she couldn't feel anything. She forced them down, and felt the fabric rip, the metal buttons falling silently into the thick rug. Another dress ruined, she thought. Everything is ruined.

Even after putting on a robe, she felt so cold. Her head pounded, just out of rhythm with the errant phone. She moved by touch and instinct into the hall, down the stairs. A light glowed from the kitchen and Erin saw her face in a mirror. She laughed. She looked like Alice Cooper, her eyes rimmed with mascara. She looked beaten. She felt beaten. I am beaten, she knew.

Maybe another drink might help. She moved to Ralph's bar. She rarely drank at home, so she had no real idea what was here.

Scotch, gin, several others, aligned around a set of glassware that she knew cost more than she made in a week. He had bought them for entertaining; the glasses she used just weren't good enough. Bastard. Scotch sounded good, so she snatched up the most expensive looking one. A glass fell onto the tiles below. It shattered with what Erin thought to be a most pleasing sound. She dropped another. Very good. It took ten minutes, but she broke them all.

Drinking from one of her glasses (a giveaway from a burger stand) she felt the rush of the whiskey move into her chest, her legs, her head. When she closed her eyes she felt as though she was floating, around and around, far above the floor. Did she have enough booze to stay this way?

She felt like calling him up, no, calling his wife up and telling her what sort of slime she bedded down with. She had met Lora once, at a cookout Tyler had hosted a few summers ago. She seemed like such a nice woman, with a head on her shoulders and a good job. It had been a nice day. She met families, kids, talked to people she had seen everyday but never really met. Tyler and Ralph had seemed to get along famously, drinking beer after beer and laughing so loud, standing in a corner of the yard. Looking back, it doesn't surprise her that they hit it off. Ralph rarely missed a chance to comment on women he saw, in a "just kidding" sort of way. He had for years, so long now that she never heard it anymore.

No, calling Lora wouldn't do. If she doesn't know about him yet it's just a matter of time, and if she did, and had decided to live with it, Erin ranting at her would just be cruel. She could call Kathy, but after what she had said at the bar Erin felt that to wake her in the middle of night with something like this would be wrong. Calling Ralph was out. She doubted if she would tell him what happened even if he were here.

She remembered the card in her purse that Adam had given her. She thought it odd at the time, and had almost thrown it out the window as she drove home. Something made her keep it. What the hell. I'll never have to see him again, and it's not like I'm inviting him over.

She dialed the number, and poured another drink as she listened to the dial tone. It rang five times, and she started to hang up. He must be out.

"Hello?"

What was she doing? Hang up, go to bed. Wake up in the morning, go to work, talk to the owner and set Tyler straight.

"Adam, it's Erin, from the restaurant? I'm sorry to wake you." She felt like an idiot.

"No, you didn't wake me. I was just watching T.V. I don't sleep much."

His voice sounded so calm, strong in the dark room. She took a drink. The floating sensation had given way to sort of throb, all through her body. She lay back on the couch, the robe falling away from her legs. Good legs, she thought, watching the dim light shift on them as she flexed her muscles.

"What's the matter?" His voice sounded like someone on a late-night radio show. She could feel the earpiece of the phone vibrate as he spoke.

"Nothing, really. I came across your card and I couldn't sleep so I called." I have to hang up. He's going to think I called because I'm horny, to make him come over. She sat quiet for a moment, while she tried to recall his face. Strong, good features. The hair. She took another drink.

"Erin, please. It's two in the morning. He called, didn't he?" They sat in silence. How did he know?

Quietly. "Yes."

"And it was bad, wasn't it?"

Again. "Yes."

"Tell me about it." She felt like he would wait on the phone until the sun came up, until she told him.

She spoke, haltingly at first but as the anger resurfaced she began to get heated, until she was crying and gulping at her drink. He listened, and never interrupted, until she finished.

"How long has this been going on?"

"About two years, give or take."

"And your husband thinks you should quit, right?"

"Yeah." She could see the piles of broken glass on the floor. It made her smile. "He thinks I'm overreacting."

"Because he can understand Tyler's point of view easier than yours, most likely."

For the second time since she had met him she got an odd feeling that he knew what she was thinking. Not a mind reading sort of thing, more like empathy.

"I guess you're right. He and Tyler have a lot of similar traits." Like treating me like a piece of flesh, to start. "I just wish he would stop, and leave me alone."

"He's never to going to stop. You are going to have to make him stop." He sounded forceful and direct.

"I can't. He wouldn't listen to me, I know." How many times had she thought of calling him on it, only to back down, and try to overlook it?

"The time for talking might be over, Erin."

She felt uneasy. She didn't want to think about that. She had imagined such horrible things.

"You know what you want. You know how you want him to feel, don't you?" He could hear her nod and went on. "You want him to do more than stop, don't you. You want him to hurt, the way he hurt you. To wake up under the same cloud that you do, don't you?"

"Yes. Yes I do." She felt hot, sweaty. Another drink, gone in an instant.

"You want to feel good again. You want control. Over your life, your body, your thoughts."

"How? I can't do that. I wouldn't know what to do." She felt on the edge, trying not to voice the things she had lived with for so long, that crowded her head.

"I do, Erin. It's my job."

CHAPTER 9

Deep down, Banks felt that the investigation was as good as over. True, it would continue for a few more months in the official sense, but after that everyone would move on to other, newer cases. After being on the force as long as he had, he knew that if they hadn't caught the guy within a couple of weeks they would never catch him unless he did it again. It had happened to him and every other detective he had known.

He had talked at length with Williams down in Florida, chased the trail of the white van until it came up empty. He re-questioned witnesses and even got the kid back in who had seen the guy. Nothing moved. The case was cold, and he knew that his work was about over. It frustrated him. Maybe it was time to pack it up, take his pension, move on to easier work that wouldn't keep him up at night.

Still, as he drove his unmarked car up Peachtree Street, looking at the faces of the people he wondered, how did it happen? How could somebody walk in a crowded place, knife another person, walk off and nobody see a thing? He looked again at the faces that passed in front of the car as he sat at a light. It could be any one of them.

He knew, of course, that he was dealing with a special sort of madness. This was not a random attack of passion or opportunity. No money was taken, no one else was touched. It looked like a hit. For what purpose? Who wanted him dead? Who had they hired to do it, and how? The person who did it was one of two things, Nelson felt. Either he was a pro, someone who had done enough of these things to gain over time a sense of invisibility. He imagined it happened to everyone who was extremely good at their job, a sense of being able to do no wrong. It was not a feeling his job could ever give him, however. Not with cases like this.

The second option was worse. The man was a sociopath, who wasn't bound by the same feelings as other humans. He had seen this once, when he was just out of college, and starting on the job. His dad had been a cop in Chicago, and had been an investigator on the John Wayne Gacy case. Banks still kept a crime scene photo that shows his dad in the background, the foreground filled with the decomposed torso of a man being pulled from under the floorboards of Gacy's comfortable suburban house. It was that case, the things he had seen, that made his father quit the force. Nelson had been twenty-five then, a beat patrolman in the Atlanta. He listened to his father's trembling voice on the phone describing the things they had learned from the interviews with Gacy. It had scared him.

He learned that there are people walking the streets, holding jobs, who are madmen. They can look just like anyone else, act like everyone else, do the same things as normal people. But inside their heads they are always looking, pondering, hunting. Maybe it was voices, or imagined demons, but something inside made them regard all they met as potential victims. He hoped that this guy, whoever he was wasn't like that, because they rarely got caught.

Banks glanced at his watch. Lunch time, or close enough. He turned off Peachtree and headed for the Varsity. This was one of the high points of living in Atlanta. Generations of people had stood at the long chrome counter and ordered junk food, watched television in the glass-walled rooms. He ordered his food and walked up to the last section of tables. A soap opera played over a sign admonishing patrons not to change the channel. He started to eat without looking at the screen.

Two bites into his chili dog his beeper shrilled. He looked down and recognized the number. Stuffing a handful of fries into his mouth and gathering the hot dog he went back out to the car.

"Had to wait until I was eating, didn't ya?" He spoke, trying to wash down what little food he had eaten with a Frosted Orange.

"For sure. I think you want to come in, see what we got." Maxwell sounded almost happy, not an emotion one finds often in their work.

"What's up?" Nelson asked, wiping chili off of his shirt. Damn.

"Remember Erin Welch, one of the witnesses from the food court?"

"Yeah, I talked to her last month sometime. She remember something else?" This would be news, seeing as how she didn't really give us anything the first time.

"No, more than that. She met the guy again."

"She what? How would she know? I thought she didn't get a good look at him. Did she see somebody on the street that reminded her of him?" Nelson was unimpressed. Some witnesses vowed that they saw people all the time. It rarely worked out.

"Better than that. She thinks she hired him. To do her boss."

Banks hit the lights on his car and wheeled out onto North Avenue.

"You got her there?" He asked as he swerved to miss a Marta bus.

"Yeah, she's in custody."

"For what?"

"Commission to commit a felony. You won't believe what the hell happened to her boss."

CHAPTER 10

From where Banks and Maxwell sat they could watch Welch through the window of the detective's area. She was hunched over a table, her arms around herself in a protective gesture. She looked pale and frightened. Staring down at the photos in his hand, Nelson imagined she would.

It was hard to tell what the pictures represented. It was a person in a hospital bed, with the top of his head covered in bandages. The eyes were covered with what looked like small white pillows. The skin around them was bright red, like sunburn. It was the result of battery acid. Another swatch of bandages wrapped around the neck. Under them, he knew, was a gash made when the victim's larynx was cut out. The splints on the hands made it look like that Freddy Kruger guy from the movies. The fingers had sustained over a dozen breaks, the result of being slammed with a heavy object. Probably a baseball bat, he thought.

"What the fuck is this?" Nelson tossed the pictures back on the desk and looked up at his partner.

"Victim is Tyler Stevens, forty-one. Works at the same office as the suspect, Erin Welch. Seems he was out at a local titty bar for most of the evening. Nobody saw him leave. They found him in the parking lot an hour or so after closing, back behind a dumpster. Looks like somebody worked him over pretty good."

"No shit. Was it a robbery?"

"No, he still had his wallet with about fifty bucks in it, all in ones." Maxwell saw his partner's look of puzzlement.

"One dollar bills - tips, for the dancers? You need to get out more, Nelson." He said, laughing.

"See what it gets you? No thanks, I'll stay at home." He motioned to the room, and Erin. "What's she doing here?"

"When somebody at work told her about Tyler she fainted. Her friend Kathy called 911 and when they were checking her out she started talking about it being her fault, that she told Adam to do it."

"Adam, who's Adam?" Nelson rubbed his eyes.

"Some guy she met in a bar. She says she called him after she had some sort of trouble with her boss on the phone. Claims that he told her he could take care of it for her. She's convinced that he was the guy in the mall."

The two men walked into the room with Welch. Banks made sure the photos of the victim were inside the folder. He sat down and looked across the table at her.

"Is he dead?"

"Did you want him to be?" Nelson asked, measuring out his words, taking his time.

"God no! I didn't want anything to happen, at least nothing like that." She asked for a cigarette. Maxwell gave her one, pulled an ashtray from a drawer and slid it in front of her. She sat holding the cigarette, staring at it.

"I haven't smoked in seven years. Said I never would again."

"We all do, trust me. Need a match?" Nelson was trying to be helpful. She kept on like she didn't hear.

"Seven years. It was the hardest thing I ever did, quitting. Took forever. I knew if I could do that I could do anything, you know?" Her eyes looked sad, far away.

"Go on."

"The last year, it's been so hard. Everyday, the same thing. Even before I got to work, I'd have to think about it, make sure not to dress the wrong way. Nothing too tight, low cut, things like that. Then all through the day he would be there, hovering, staring, leering at me." She tried to light the cigarette. Maxwell had to steady her hand so she could. She inhaled and the skin on her face flushed pink, and she coughed.

"Damn, I feel dizzy." She stubbed it out in the ashtray.

Nelson spoke, as gently as he could. "What happened the other night? You mentioned a phone call?" He looked back at the report folder. The statement sheet was stapled to the front.

"Tyler called me at home and harassed me. It freaked me out."

"You say he harassed you." Nelson started to say more but she stopped him.

"You say. Is that a delicate way of saying nothing happened? Why would I lie? Ask Kathy! She knows what the hell he has been doing. Ask him! He can't deny it!" Her shoulders shook. She seemed to be on the verge of sobbing, but too proud to break down.

"I'm sure my partner didn't mean anything, mam. That's just the way we are trained to talk. Just tell us what happened, and about this man Adam. Adam Winter, you said his name was?" She seemed to loosen listening to Maxwell. He was better with witnesses, always had been. Nelson was better with facts, leads, and theories. They fit well together. It was a form of good cop, bad cop. Sometimes it worked.

"I went with Kathy to a restaurant near the office."

"What was it called, do you remember?"

"Rio Bravo, the mexican place on Windy Hill?" Maxwell nodded as he made notes.

"Kathy had to leave and when I turned around there was a man sitting next to me. I hadn't heard him come up and it surprised me." Nelson interrupted her.

"Was the bar crowded?"

"How do you mean?" She felt confused.

"What I'm getting at, was the seat next to you the only one open in the place, or do you think he just took the first one he came to?"

"Well, we were sitting pretty far back. He would have had to walk down most of the bar to get to where we were. I think that there had been some other places free before ours." As she spoke it started to clear in her head what he was saying.

"Do you think he was following me?" She didn't want to think about that.

"What makes you think this was the man you saw at the mall? In your statement you said that you thought the man at the mall was short with curly hair. You say this Adam person is taller, with straight black hair. You see the problem?" Nelson was getting tired of this. He wasn't sure what had happened, or how she tied into it all. It was frustrating.

"I just had a feeling, later, when I talked to him on the phone. I know this will sound crazy, but I got a real clear mental image of him when he talked. It just came into my head, when he was telling me about what he would do to Tyler. I knew it was him. It was like a voice in the background, saying 'you know I can, don't you?' It was creepy."

"What made you keep talking to him?" Phillip looked up and spoke. "Did he threaten you?"

Erin remembered the flush of her body when he talked to her. When he told her how he would handle Tyler, and how she would be free, in power. She had felt a rush of relief, like a release, stronger than she had ever felt. She had woken up on the couch the next morning, late for work. Her ear had throbbed from holding the phone, her body sore, still tired.

"No, he didn't threaten me, or try to scare me. You have to understand I was desperate. I didn't have anyone else to talk to. He just seemed to understand right off what I was trying to say."

"You are married, right?" Phillip was checking her statement.

"Yes."

"Did you tell your husband about the phone call from your boss?"

"No. He was out of town on business." She stopped short of saying anything else.

"Did he know of your ongoing problems with Tyler?"

"Not much. I didn't feel that it would do any good. He didn't really want me to work in the first place. He would have wanted me to quit, or get another job and just go on like nothing happened."

"So you hadn't mentioned the call to him at all?" Nelson looked a little shocked.

"No, and if you don't understand it I don't think I could make you. You just had to be there. What's going to happen to me now? Am I going to be arrested?" She looked scared again.

"Well, first off, we need to find this man Adam. Do you know where he is staying, any way to get in touch with him?" Nelson turned over a new page in his notebook.

"He said he was in town for a few days on business. Said he was going to Miami after here, I think. He gave me a card." She reached into her purse and handed it to him.

Nelson looked at the white piece of paper in disbelief. He hadn't heard of killers using business cards before.

CHAPTER 11

It was so easy to blend in. Adam sat at the counter, nursing a cup of coffee, waiting for the men to show up. It was ten minutes before they were scheduled to meet, but he wanted to watch them come in, make sure that it was just the two of them. They had described themselves, but Adam felt that it wasn't going to be necessary. They would be easy enough to pick out. He was equally sure that they would never guess who he was. He had a white T-shirt on, jeans. His hair was tucked up into a baseball cap that carried the logo of a beer company. He looked around the diner again, back at the door. They walked in, looked around as they spoke to the hostess. As they got seated in a booth he looked them over.

Both were balding, and going to gray. Cheap suit on the taller one, the other had a button-up plaid shirt with sunglasses stuck in the pocket. The guy in the suit checked his watch, sipped coffee. The other dumped packet after packet of sugar in a tall glass of iced tea. They looked up from menus as he walked over.

"You Kern?" He said to the guy in the suit. The man nodded, motioned for the other to move over, let Adam sit down. He did.

"So, you ready to help us?" The younger man drank a gulp of his tea, made a face, shook in more sugar. Real sugar, not even NutraSweet.

Adam looked over at his seatmate.

"You should slow down on that stuff, it's poison."

The man cocked his head and laughed, "Poison. Now that's funny, coming from a guy like you." He kept laughing until Adam spoke.

"Let's get this straight. You don't know what kind of guy I am, and I don't care what kind of guy you are. But if you talk like that again, I'll reach under this table and break your kneecap with my hand." Adam laid his hand on the man's knee and squeezed. He felt the muscles in the thigh tighten and then start to quiver. "You'll never walk a straight line again. Understand?"

The other man spoke sharply.

"Just shut up, Frank. We need to get out of here, let the man do his job." He looked over at Adam. "So everything's a go?"

"Sure," Adam answered, putting his hands back on the tabletop. Frank reached down to his knee, rubbing it.

"The flight's coming in at 9:15, gate D, number 111. It shouldn't be too hard to pick them out, they all will be wearing bow-ties. Guess they think it makes them look like professors or something." The man chuckled at the idea. "You know who this guy is?" He asked to Adam.

"No. Don't really see how it matters. Tell me if you want. I don't care." He shooed the waitress away, leaned back in the booth.

"I guess you're right. Name's the Reverend Conner Simpson. At least that's his given name. Goes by some Muslim shit now, some African sounding crap."

"Yeah, I heard of him. From D.C., right? What's he ever done to you?" Not that he really cared, but he wanted to see what sort of situation he was dealing with, if they were serious. You had to be careful, sometimes they got cold feet, backed out. Better they do it now instead of later, running to the cops and trying to turn him in. He thought about Erin, wondering if that had been a mistake.

"We own a series of plants all over the country. Kern-Warner? We make a little bit of everything, from heavy machinery to outboard motors."

"So what does this have to do with Simpson?" Adam looked at the clock over the door. About an hour and a half before the plane was due.

"He has some sort of action group called the Harvest Coalition, and they are picketing our factories, offices. Claim we don't have enough blacks and minorities in our corporate and management levels. His lawyers are saying that they are going to file suit in Federal court, that they have a group of former employees that we fired, just because they are black." The man's voice was getting heated. "It had nothing to do with them being black. Dammit, this is my company. I can hire and fire who the fuck I want, right?" He looked at Adam.

"I wouldn't know. So what's the worst this guy can do? Cause a stink, a little bad press?"

"We are in the process of being bought out by a Japanese firm. They have let us know that if we don't seem able to conduct our business out of the public eye then they will go elsewhere. We're talking big money, you understand? I need that money." The man sounded desperate, and as he reached into his coat pocket his hand fluttered.

"Speaking of money, here it is." He started to pull out something.

"Don't be a jerk," Adam hissed. "Give that to me later, outside."

The man took his hand out of the suit coat, and nodded his head yes. "So you will shoot him at the airport?"

Adam looked around at the other booths. Most were empty, and in the ones that weren't people kept on eating, not looking up.

"You're as stupid as your friend here. Just shut the fuck up and wait till we leave, all right? Let's go." Adam stood.

Frank looked up from the table. "We're leaving? I thought we were going to eat. I'm starved."

The taller man looked down. "We'll get something on the way back to the office. This man has to get going, right?"

"Yeah. I'll be in the white van. Follow me in your car until I stop, okay?" This wasn't working out right. These guys would talk, he bet. He considered pulling out and saying no go, but he needed the money. He had to get rid of the van, get back home to New Orleans.

"Gotcha." The man picked up the check and Adam waited until they were on their way to the register before he started walking. Frank was limping, he could see. Adam smiled. He still had good hand strength.

He started up the van and checked the side-view mirror. They were in a dark red car, a sedan. He pulled out of the parking lot and drove three or four miles, stopping at a parking lot for a mini-mall. Hundreds of cars, nobody would see them. Hide in light, as always.

He walked up to the car, got in the back. The man handed him an envelope. Adam stuck it in his back pocket without looking at it.

"You not going to count it?" Frank spoke, with a look of amazement on his face.

"I'm not the kind of guy you would want to stiff, am I Frank?" Adam looked straight at his face. The men stared for a moment, and Frank broke it off first. Turning back to the front of the car he said he guessed not.

"So like I was saying, you gonna shoot him at the airport?" The other man said, his fingers tapping nervously on the seat back.

"Never said I was going to shoot him. You did. You just told me to take him out. I figure how I do it is my own business."

"What do you mean? If you don't shoot him, what are you going to do?" The man looked confused.

"You don't carry a gun into an airport. You shoot somebody, everybody around freezes, starts looking at everyone else. You have to walk away somehow." Adam knew that he could, but he decided to do it another way, just to make sure. "You want to set it up so that when it happens, you are long gone. That way there's no chance of some trigger-happy bodyguard or airport security man blowing your head off. Follow me?"

"He's talking about a bomb, Mr. Kern." Frank was catching on quick Adam thought. "I'm right, aren't I?" He was looking scared, and wiped sweat off of his forehead. "We didn't say nothing about no bomb. Do you have any idea what a bomb could do at a busy place like that? Shit, the Atlanta airport is one of the most crowded in the world! Do you know what something like that would do?" Frank looked at the other man in the front seat. So did Adam.

"Yeah, I do." He pulled the envelope out of his pocket, set it on the back of the seat, where Kern could get it. "You want out, say so. I walk away, no questions." He stared at the man.

He waited a moment before speaking. Adam could hear the cars pass around them, the honk of a horn.

"I take it you've done this before." The voice was flat, emotionless.

Adam didn't speak for awhile. He looked at both of the men, around at the car, sizing them up.

"Open your shirts." Frank started to protest, but the driver started loosening his tie, unbuttoning his shirt.

He looked over at Frank and said, "Do it. He wants to see if we are wearing a wire. Hurry up." In a moment both men's bare chests were exposed. Adam nodded, told them to get dressed.

"It doesn't matter if I have or haven't. You called me, remember? I imagine that I came recommended." At this point, it was up to them. Adam could take it or leave it.

"Highly." It was the driver. He handed the envelope back to Adam. "Do what you think is best. One nigger or ten, it doesn't make a difference to me."

Adam nodded and took the envelope.

"Gotta go. Gotta meet a plane."

CHAPTER 12

He drove the van down Buford Highway, checking the bag on the floorboard beside him. It was a soft-sided carry-on, and Adam knew that hundreds of people at the airport would be carrying ones just like it. He made the exit to the interstate and switched on the radio. It was the morning edition of NPR. He caught it mid-story.

"The FBI has released a report showing that gang activity in the United States has risen fifty percent in the last three years. Gangs started in the Los Angeles area have spread into other parts of the country, as far away as the Washington, D.C. area." Adam remembered the riots, and knew that he saw the same sort of faces here. A lot of the signs around the diner where he had met the men earlier had been in Spanish, and two teens sitting at the counter beside Adam had black diamond tattoos on the third knuckle of their left hands, a gang ID he figured.

The woman's voice on the radio continued. "One of the new items in the FBI report is the accounting of gang and gang-related activities in places not normally thought to be havens for such. From our sister station in Ames, Indiana, here is Thomas Harper with a report."

Adam switched off the radio and pushed a CD into the player. Bach filled the van and his head. Soon they would be everywhere, these children of the darkness. It is inevitable. He wondered how long it would take, how many futile gestures would be made before the end became apparent. Little steps, like the ban on assault rifles made scant difference, and even those were hard won victories. America was a land unlike any he had ever been in. Other nations didn't allow the same freedoms we did, and they dealt with most crimes in a swifter, less passionate manner. They were used to terrorism, acts like the one he was about to do. If he were to set off a bomb in a European airport it would not be unexpected. But here, in America, they had never faced something like that. He wondered what the reaction would be.

He pulled into the lane marked long-term parking, and slowed as the line of cars before him came to a near stop. Frank had been right, this place was packed. Most seemed to be businessmen, rushing from one hotel room to another. Like him. He parked the van away from the other cars and looked around inside before leaving. He wasn't planning on coming back to it. He gathered up the tape from the dash and picked up the bag from the floor.

He knew that no one who saw him striding across the parking lot would ever remember him. He looked just like hundreds of others. He walked under the overhangs that marked the entrance to the airport. He looked up at the signs until he found Delta. Walking into the airport he was assaulted by a vast roar of noise, going up to the high glass ceiling overhead. He kept walking past the baggage claim until he found the arrival and departure board. He looked for the 9:15 flight from Washington. On time, the sign said, and he looked at it for a few minutes, watching the lines change. He glanced at his watch. Ten after. He walked down the terminal and got to the trains and marveled at the idea of a building being so huge that you had to have a train system inside to move people around. He stepped on one and moved to the back. The car filled quickly, and he set his bag at his feet, between himself and the wall. He didn't want somebody knocking into it, and starting off the reaction.

It was quiet, just the rushing of the unit as it burrowed into the darkness. Most of the people were in suits, men and women on their way to conduct business who knows where. Near the door a woman sat with two children. She was dark haired and attractive, even if she looked a little frazzled by minding the kids.

"Can we ride the train back?" The boy said in a squeal.

"I want to ride the moving sidewalk! You promised, Mom!" The little girl's face squenched up in a pout as she looked up at her mother.

"Lets just worry about meeting your father, okay? Maybe we'll let him choose." The children quieted down, and stared out the windows. The train grew silent again.

The ride was fast, and soon they were there, the train lurching to a stop. A voice came out of the ceiling, a monotone telling them they had reached terminal D and to be careful departing. Adam waited until most of the others had filed out the doors and then he followed, glimpsing the gate far down the crowded area. He walked past hordes of returning travelers, thousands of people from all around the world. He loved airports. Watching the planes, looking at the people, he could sit for hours before the huge windows, watching the jets land and take off, watch them taxi up to the terminal, the accordion-like ramps moving up to them like snakes.

He waited at the arrival area for the flight. It looked like it had been crowded. After the others had gotten out, met those who were waiting for them, Adam began to wonder if he had been given the wrong information, or if the Reverend had opted to stay put, or go somewhere else.

Soon, however, a line of serious looking black men came up the hallway from the plane. Kern had been right. They all had on bow ties. The ones at the front were muscle, and their eyes swept back and forth over the room, looking for whatever they were trained to see. Bringing up the rear were more bow ties, these older. They were bunched around a man with short hair, going gray so that it looked like snow on the dark head. This must be him.

Adam got up and started walking back down the corridor. He knew where they were going. He thought about the little girl and her comment about a moving sidewalk. He stepped onto it and could see them, a family now. The father held the girl on his hip, and the boy was holding up a T-shirt as he rode, a present from the father. They looked happy, the mother's head resting on the man's shoulder as they rode.

Delta was in trouble, laying off people, but you wouldn't know from watching the baggage area. The long silver conveyers, five or six of them, were crowded by masses of people, watching, reaching for bags. Redcaps milled around the terminal entrance, with push carts at the ready. Adam waited until the group of black men arrived. The muscle moved over to wait for the bags. The Reverend seemed almost asleep as he sat on a chair against the wall. Adam spotted more of the group at a bank of phones beside him. As the younger men began to load a hand-truck with bags he walked outside, and stopped near the limousine waiting there. The trunk was open, and one of the men began tossing bags into it. Behind it was a van, and most of the men got into that. Adam looked up, over the cars to the lanes of traffic pulling in, as if he was waiting for someone to meet him. He looked down at the bag beside him, and moved out of the way when a voice behind said, "Excuse me." He looked at the back of Simpson's head as he ducked down to get into the long white car. Adam looked back up at the cars coming into the area, and waved as though he saw someone he recognized. The limousine trunk was still open, but nobody was around. He walked past it, eyes focused on a car he picked out in the line. As he neared the back of the limo he swung his bag hard against the front of a pushcart, and heard the glass jar inside break. He tossed the bag into the trunk of the car and looked back to a man in a bow tie, struggling with a pair of suitcases, trying to get them into the van.

"You all finished here? We gotta get this area cleared out, let the other cars in." The man with the bags looked over, annoyed at the redcap standing behind the limo, his hand on the trunk.

"Yeah, we're almost done. Just give us a second."

"Sure. You want me to shut this?" He motioned at the trunk lid.

"Yeah, thanks." The man hoisted the bags into the sliding door of the van, and Adam shut the trunk and walked away from the car, toward the parking lots.

He walked up the stairs, and turned at the top, near the lip of the parking lots and looked back at the door. People milled around, and Adam saw the family from the train, father burdened under the weight of his overnight bag on one side, his daughter on the other. The limo sat idling in place, and someone slid the doors shut on the van. Adam walked down the parking lot and knocked on the door of the first cab in a long line.

"Where you headed, mister?" The cabbie spoke, looking up from a newspaper.

"Swissotel, the one near Lenox?"

"Sure." The cabbie looked at him, and spoke again. "Where're your bags?"

"Idiots lost them. Maybe you can drop me at the mall instead of the hotel, let me pick up some stuff until they find my suitcase." He opened the back door of the cab and sat down.

"Hope you have better luck than my wife." The cab pulled into the departing cars, ready for the highway.

"How's that?" Adam knew it would be about three minutes more before the acid from the broken glass melted the cover around the lump of plastic explosive in the trunk of the limo. The cab moved forward, about even with the road.

"Wife went last summer up to Maine, to see her sister? When she got there, her bags were gone. We didn't get them back for two months. Told us they went to Paris! Got loaded on the wrong cart, they said. You were right, those people are idiots. No wonder they all go out of business, treating people like that."

The driver merged onto the highway, and the road rose above and around the airport. Adam looked back at the terminal, but he couldn't see the limo in the line of cars leaving.

"You mind if I play the radio? Rush is on, talking about the president." Adam had no idea who Rush was. He moved over in the seat and looked out the back window.

"Sure, go ahead."

The man was reaching for the knob on the radio when the ground under their wheels shook. He whipped his head around, slowing the cab. A great wall of flame and smoke rose over the airport, like orange and gray rain falling up. "What the fuck was that!" The man tried to watch the road and the fire at the same time.

"Hell if I know." Adam spoke, his mind filled with an image of a small girl on a moving sidewalk.

CHAPTER 13

All over the world, wherever there was a television set, people sat quiet as they stared at the screen. The pictures changed, the voices of the announcers varied in language, but the basic image was the same. Hartsfield airport, second busiest in the world, was on fire. Banks watched from his living room in southeast Atlanta. He was ten minutes away from the blaze. Looking out his back window earlier he could see the smoke.

He poured more Wild Turkey into a glass and turned up the volume. He watched the commentator on CNN talk, as he had all day.

"At this hour the fire is still only partially contained. Firefighters are attempting to head off the blaze before it can reach the underground gas storage tanks at the rear of the airport. We have learned that another jet, this one from USAir, has exploded, for a total of five. Now to Bernard Shaw, for a recap of today's events." The woman turned to a man sitting next to her at the desk.

"Thank you, Kimberley. At approximately 9:30 this morning a large explosion rocked Hartsfield Airport in Atlanta, Georgia. The blast is now thought to have been triggered from a large amount of plastic explosive in the rear of a limousine that contained the Reverend Conner Simpson. Reverend Simpson was in Atlanta to attend the annual ceremony at the King Center. The death toll stands at this moment at 287 persons, although this figure is expected to rise as soon as firefighters say that the fire is contained enough for rescue efforts. We have film shot from a helicopter early this morning that contains footage of the explosion." The screen went black for a moment, and then was filled with the face of man wearing a headset, the skyline of Atlanta behind him. He was adjusting the microphone at his neck, talking to a second person in the helicopter. As he straightened his shirt and smoothed his hair, readying himself for an on-air traffic report, Nelson watched the image from the camera lurch and the helicopter drop as the sound of a hundred cannons filled the air. The picture swerved crazily for a few minutes, and finally came to rest on the airport. Banks could see the heat shimmering, making the building look underwater.

He leaned forward and looked closely at the screen, even though he had seen this footage about ten times already today. The entire front of the terminal, which he guessed was about as long as two football fields, was in flames. The large windows that rose from the floor up to form a ceiling had fallen into the middle of the lobby. The right side of the atrium looked swollen, as if it was holding back water. It blew out a moment later, and flames roared across the parking lots, igniting everything but the stone of the structure.

All around the picture were hundreds of bodies, most with pockets of flame dancing on them. At the center of the blaze he could almost make out the frame of the limo that the bomb had been in. The helicopter rode higher, bumpy from the heat, across the airport to the runways. A plane had crashed, Nelson guessed, when the bomb went off. He had spoken to his next door neighbor when he got home this morning and the man said he had felt the bomb go off here, over five miles away. The plane on the runway looked as if a huge child had flung it to the ground in a rage. The ground crews and the fire wagons were swarming around it already, although he didn't see how anything could have survived that. The film ran on, showing a few more scenes from the blast, and then Shaw came back on the television.

"Government officials have no leads on who set the bomb, and state that no terrorist organization has taken credit for the attack. This is the first such assault in the United States since the World Trade Center bombing, and one that many have felt was a long time coming. Here with this part of the story is Jefferson Pack from our Washington office."

Nelson switched off the television and sat in the fading light of the day. He felt somewhat responsible for the attack, in a strange way. It had happened in his city, in his backyard. He knew that Atlanta police had attempted to provide security for Simpson and his party, but had been rebuffed. A person with the public persona of a Reverend Simpson attracted numerous death threats, and had dealt with them all internally until now.

He knew that the investigation of the bombing would be a national or international process, and the local cops would be shut out of the loop. Fine with him. He had his own crazy to deal with.

He rose from the living room and went to the small room he kept as a study. When he bought the house he told himself that the room would make a fine sewing room for the future Mrs. Banks. Over the years he had slowly moved his own belongings into it, a computer and some pictures from the force. He still didn't feel that it was his room. Outside the window he could see the small creek that bordered his property. Years ago he would sit out there and drink a beer, watching the sun go down. Now the rocks that edged the trickle of water were covered in obscene graffiti and what little flow there had been was clogged with condoms and crack vials. The first time he had walked across his yard and heard the familiar crunch of glass he went out and had burglar bars put on his windows.

It made him angry that he should have to live as a prisoner in his home. It was enough, he felt, to carry the things he did in his head, day after day, until he became numb. But every night he pulled into his driveway and saw the bars that looked eerily like the ones on the holding cells downtown. He wanted to keep on driving.

He sat at the computer and logged on to COPNET, a bulletin board for law enforcement officers around the country. He had two messages in his in-box. The first was from his father's old partner, Howard Bain. He hadn't thought of him in years, and hadn't seen him since his father's funeral, five years ago. He clicked to open the message.

Nelson, thought you might have missed this because of the bombing but Gacy was executed by lethal injection at 7:33 this morning. I only wish your dad was here to see his work pay off. Let me know how you're doing.

Howard

Although Howard didn't mention it, Banks could see the cop sense of justice at work. Gacy was convicted on thirty-three counts of first-degree murder, and so he died at 7:33. It gave the whole horrible affair a sense of completion. Howard was right, his dad would have liked to be there, to watch Gacy's eyes flutter and close as the chemicals seeped into his blood. He wondered what thoughts had gone through the mind of a monster as it lay stretched out on the table, arms and legs strapped down and the feeling of numbness overtake him. Nelson would doubt it was remorse, because the man had spent thirteen years on death row. The time for pity had long passed. From what his father had told him about Gacy's mind he imagined that he must have felt like he was getting off easy, only having to die. He was.

The second message was from Williams in Florida. Since talking with him about the campus murders, they had been swapping notes back and forth on the net for weeks. Most of the time it was just to shoot the shit, let off steam. Sometimes the two exchanged info. He called the message up.

Your last mail sounded as if you were about to throw in the towel on your food court guy. I think this might help. The last couple of weeks we have been seeing reports of people robbed or shot by gangs. When we talk to witnesses we keep getting conflicting information, much like you. The only thing they seem to agree on is the fact that the gangs were teenagers. After that, white, black, PR, who knows. I don't think this is a matter of different peoples recall here. I think somehow, by disguise or what, I don't know, these kids are changing their basic makeup. Give me a call and I'll fill you in more.

Later, J.

This sounded a lot like the ideas that Nelson had been kicking around in his head. Of course it wasn't the sort of thing you could bounce around the squad room over coffee, but all other attempts to reason this thing didn't pan out. He'd give Williams a call in the morning, when he had the file in front of him. He was just too tired tonight.

CHAPTER 14

The Masquerade Club was located in the remains of an old grain mill. It rose three stories in the air, and retained the feel of an abandoned warehouse or factory. It sat on the edges of both downtown Atlanta and the Virginia-Highlands residential district. Seven days a week it was a haven for the city's youth, with live bands and industrial music. It was known as a place where you could find anything at any hour of the day or night. The crowd ranged from beer-drinking college boys to leather freaks. A person could wander from floor to floor and be solicited with everything from pot to heroin, and if you asked the right person you could buy everything from a car stereo (fresh out of the parking lot) to a stolen handgun.

Robert Morris leaned back against the bar and exhaled smoke, watching a pair of girls dance to Nine Inch Nails, the sound pounding from speakers hanging around the room. A layer of sweat and smoke drifted up until the room felt like a sauna. Morris watched the girls a little longer, and decided they were dykes. Figures.

"So what's the story? We gonna deal or what?" The boy was starting to piss Robert off. He didn't want to sell him a gun, but money was money and this kid, who looked fresh out of high school was talking cash. Of course Robert wasn't but about three years out of school himself, if you looked on his driver's license. If you looked at his face you would go five years older than that.

"You got the two hundred?" Morris asked the boy, half-hoping he'd say no.

"Yeah, but that's a lot of money for something I really just want to rent. You sure I can't just use it for awhile, bring it back?"

"Yeah, borrow a piece, smoke somebody and give it back to me? Do I look that fucking stupid? I might as well have it done myself, at least I know that I wouldn't have the cops pounding on my door in the middle of the night," Robert snorted.

"Hey," the boy said, "that's cool. You know somebody that would do it? How much?"

Robert thought about it a minute, looking at the kid. What the hell would he want somebody dead for? Comes down to it, doesn't really matter, one reason's as good as another.

"Same price. $200. Cash. And you have to show me where this guy lives. You can find the place?"

"Hell yes, I've known the fucker since I was a kid."

"So what did he ever do to you?"

"Clown moved on my girl when I was out of town, working for my dad you know? I go and talk to the dude, and he gets riled, so he sends his boys out after me, they beat the piss out of me. I ain't takin' that kind of shit." The boy looked defiant.

"Sounds like your buddy the one doing all the taking, you ask me."

The kid pushed away from the bar with a hot look in his eyes.

"Hey, fuck you man! I ain't gonna take no trash off of you either, it ain't like you done me any favors." The boy's face was red and Robert handed him a beer, to cool him down.

"Take it easy, just observing. You want this thing done, I think I can handle it. You ready to roll?" He imagined the kid would fade on him, come up with a few good reasons to put it off, and that would be the end of it.

"Sure, let's get out of here. You got the heat?"

"You wanna say that a little louder? Maybe those guys on the other wall didn't hear you." This kid was a real pain in the ass. "Pay for the drinks and let's go." Robert moved toward the stairs and the boy caught up.

They didn't speak until they had left the building. Robert's ears buzzed from the pressure of the music in the club that made the crunch of his boots on the gravel parking lot sound like he was walking in socks, not Doc Martens.

"You got a car?" Robert asked. The kid pointed to a ragged out Datsun against a chain link fence. They got in and drove.

"This gonna be a long ride?" Robert asked. He wanted to get back to the club, see if the two girls had split up yet.

"Not very. Here, hold the wheel." Robert reached over and steadied the car as the kid held a glass pipe up to his mouth. He picked a few white rocks out of a wad of foil in his lap and dropped them in the bowl of the pipe, holding a lighter underneath until the gum in the crack began to boil and smoke. He dropped the lighter and inhaled deep, closing his eyes.

"Damn, watch the road! You gonna get the wrong guy killed, you keep doing that shit."

"Cool. Want some?" He handed the pipe over and Robert relit it and sucked in. The cloud rolled into his lungs and his brain, numbing them. No wonder he made so much money selling rock. This feels nice.

"Thanks. What's your name, anyway?"

"Kenny. Mind some tunes?" He pushed a tape into the deck and turned up the volume. Cypress Hill pulsed through the car. Dope music for dope times.

"It's just up here, at the corner."

"Park the car back here, away from that street light. You think he's home?" There were no lights on in the house, but a pickup truck was in the driveway.

"Yeah. He's up there. So you know how to get here, you gonna tell the guy where to go?" Kenny filled the pipe again.

"What guy? We're gonna do this thing now. You got the money?" Robert pulled the gun out from his waistband and checked the load. Ready to go.

"What? I ain't gonna be here! Asshole knows me." The boy looked scared.

"What do you think, he's gonna call 911 when we leave? We walk in, bam, we leave. You can stay in the car if you want, but I ain't spending all fucking night out here. Gimme that pipe."

Robert smoked some more and felt strong. Kenny reached into his sock and pulled out a roll of bills. He peeled off four and handed them to Morris, leaving a lot left over.

"Nice chunk of change. Daddy pay well?" Robert thought Kenny looked like a little rich kid.

"Don't pay shit. Course he does leave a lot of money lying around and you know how hard finding good help is these days." Kenny laughed and put the money back.

Robert got out of the car and moved across the street, keeping his eye on the house. The crack made him feel like he was riding an electric wave. No sign of a dog, and the lights were out in all the other houses along the street.

Keeping his voice low he whispered to Kenny.

"He alone in there, or does he have roommates?"

"Nah, it's just him, far as I know. How we gonna get in?"

"Piece of cake. These places always have cheap locks or somebody leaves a window open. Don't worry. I'll go in, come around and unlock the door and let you in." Robert looked at the boy and waited for a response. "Unless you wanna stay back there in the car."

"Shit, might as well go in. Like you say, he ain't goin' anywhere."

Robert moved around the perimeter of the house. At the back, away from what he figured were the bedrooms, was a concrete porch leading up to a pair of sliding doors. He knelt down and lit the lighter, looking at the handle. He pulled on it once, and felt it move. Looking around and listening, he waited a moment.

When it sounded quiet he put both hands on the door and pulled with a jolt. The door slid open.

"Works every time. I used to lock myself out of the house when I was a kid. Learned to do this when I was seven. Knew it would come in handy." The breeze from outside moved the curtains at the door in and out, but otherwise the house was still. They went in, Kenny sliding the door shut behind them.

The house was dark, the only bright spot the red light of the DVD player, blinking 12:00 over and over. The house looked like every other rental house Robert had ever seen, with mismatched sofas and an orange crate filled with records. A purse lay open on a coffee table. Kenny was flipping through a wallet, reading the name on a license.

"Bitch is here." He hissed.

"Who? The one who ditched ya?"

"Yeah. She said she wasn't gonna see him again. Guess I shouldn't have trusted her, you think?"

"I never have. It's something you learn. You ready to rock and roll?"

"Yeah, I guess." Kenny's voice wavered a bit, but he followed when Robert moved into a hallway. He nodded when Robert held his finger to his mouth and pointed down the hall. Passing an empty bedroom he walked in and grabbed a pair of pillows from a bed, holding them over the barrel of the gun.

They paused at the last door and looked in. Robert could make out a vague shape in the bed. Kenny nudged him and spoke.

"Do it."

As Robert raised the gun up to his shoulder a dark haired man sat up.

"What the fuck? Kenny, what the hell are you doing?" The other figure started to move but the man pushed it down with his arm, but not before Robert saw a mane of blond hair.

"Fuckin' asshole, steal my girl and then send some of your boys after me? Smoke him, Robert!" The girl sat up, her eyes large and unblinking. She was nude, and made no attempt to cover herself.

"Kenny, this is scaring me." The girl spoke, sounding like she was about ten years old. Of course, looking at her body Robert could tell she was a lot older than that. "Kenny, who's the dude with the gun? If you wanted to scare Eddie and me you did it. Tell him to put the gun away."

Eddie looked over at Kenny and laughed. "You better do it because if I get out of this bed I'm gonna fuckin' murder you, little man." He said sneeringly.

Kenny looked over at Robert and the gun. "Do it."

Robert held a pillow up to the gun and fired. The sound was huge in the room, even with the pillow. Stuffing floated in the air and for a moment it looked like snow. The girl scrambled off the edge of the bed, her breasts splattered with blood.

"Kenny stop! Kenny make him stop!" she screamed, and cried over and over, her body convulsing. Robert looked over at Kenny.

"What about her?" Kenny held out his hand, and Robert handed over the pistol. Kenny walked until he was standing over the bed. The figure wasn't moving, and the wall behind the bed was covered in a sliding ooze of blood.

"I gave you a chance to be down with me, didn't I Rhonda? You down with me?" The girl kept crying, and Robert spoke.

"Do it or not, but we gotta book. The law is gonna show in a second."

Kenny kept the gun steady at her head. "You down with me, Rhonda?" and the gun exploded again, over and over, until it clicked empty. Robert backed out of the room, and stumbled down the hall. He made it to the car before he threw up. He'd never seen so much blood.

They drove back toward the club, stopping at some railroad tracks as Robert wadded up his bloody shirt and tossed it out the window. Kenny passed the pipe back to him. Robert smoked and leaned his head back against the seat. The industrial sound of Ministry filled the small car and mixed with the acid smell of the crack, almost like back at the club. He would skip the girls tonight. Closing his eyes, Robert could see the face of the man in the mall bathroom, long black hair hanging straight down to his shoulders. He was laughing.

CHAPTER 15

When Erin woke she lay still without opening her eyes, sustaining the idea of sleep and forestalling the start of the day. She didn't want to get up and make the trip back to the police station. Every day she had waited for the feelings of shame to lessen, and they never did. At first, in the days after the attack on Tyler, she felt guilt, and tried to tell herself that she hadn't actually caused it to happen. But the longer she lived with it the more she came to admit that she had indeed set the assault in motion, and that carried a measure of shame and anger with it.

The larger problem, however, was that there was no problem. Granted, she wouldn't have done exactly what Adam had done because she wasn't that vicious, but the fact of the matter was simple: Tyler wouldn't do it again. She had taken a stand, stood up for herself and caused the pain to stop. The fact that this caused her relief was something she didn't know she had in her.

Now she had to go back to the station, and answer the same maddening questions from Banks and Maxwell that she had already answered. She was lucky, she knew, not to be in jail. Even though she was convinced that she had as much as slammed the baseball bat onto Tyler's hands the police were more interested in catching what they considered to be a sociopath. She wished them well. The feeling she got from Adam, the way he carried himself, was one of supreme confidence. He wouldn't get caught, she knew. If he ever stopped, it would be according to his timetable and reasons, not those of a man wearing a badge.

She rose and paced the house, grateful that Ralph had left for work hours ago. He knew nothing of the whole affair. If she told him she was afraid that either he wouldn't believe it, or worse, that he would admire it. When she married him she had a vague notion that things would get more interesting and more alive as the years went on, that they would understand each other better, and she would begin to feel the emotions that other married people felt. They never had. Now she was too old or too scared to leave and start anew. She wondered if he felt the same. Or if he felt at all.

Driving to the meeting she watched the trees roll past her window. Atlanta was lovely at the beginning of spring, before the heat and humidity and bugs invaded and forced the city indoors. She loved it here, and felt aligned with the region's present and the history of it all. Ralph, transplanted from New Jersey, thought that the south started with Rhett Butler and ended after the last *Smokey and the Bandit* movie. He found the people down here too slow at most everything, and dumber than dirt. Hell, she thought, if you grew up with the kind of summers we did you'd be slow as well.

But now the south scared her. The things about the area that led her in college to read Faulkner and O'Connor, the bizarre world view that would shock her friends but that made perfect sense to her (like the mother and son in that O'Connor story about the bus ride) now made her nervous. The south had always been a violent place, full of lynching and feuds among neighbors that she never found anywhere else. Atlanta, in its scramble to become a major city, had experienced the same problems that all large, transient cities did. High murder rates, rapes and assaults were so common that they weren't even reported in the papers anymore unless the victim was famous or rich, or the act itself was noteworthy.

But more and more she could feel the undercurrent of desperation, the abandonment of the restraint that once had been an unspoken law. People were more vocal in their beliefs and that, all in all, was good. But like Erin, many people couldn't find the release or justice they sought from simple words in letters to the editor anymore. She had felt the rage around her, and in her.

She walked up the steps of the police building, cowering slightly from the din that surrounded her. The place was a madhouse; people shouting, phones ringing, and the constant background chatter of a roomful of people all talking at once. As she made her way to Banks' desk an older man seated at a table whistled at her, and when she turned and looked he held up his hands, the glint of handcuffs shining in the bad overhead lighting.

"Yo baby, what say you get these bracelets off and we have a good time, you and me?" He leered at her and she could see that his pants were half unzipped. She cringed and looked around, to see if she could see Banks or his partner, Maxwell, or anyone else that could offer a port in the storm. She was relieved to see a uniformed cop move up to the man on the bench.

"Stanley, you bothering this lady?"

"Nah, I was just saying hello. You know me, I'm a nice guy, right?" He kept darting his eyes back to Erin, with a smirk.

"One more word, Stanley and we might have to have an attitude adjustment, you understand, you drunk fuck?" The officer moved off and left the man alone at the table, quiet at least.

"You ready?" The voice of Banks from over her shoulder startled her, made her jump, but still she was glad to see him. He led her to an enclosed room, much like the one she had been in the day she had heard about Tyler.

"Sorry about the scum out there. Seems people just don't know when to shut up." He opened a notebook and laid it on the table.

"What's he here for?"

"Beat his ex-wife when she wouldn't let him see his kids last week. He gets drunk and starts a fuss almost once a month. Or at least he did."

"Did? You think he's going to stop?" Erin couldn't imagine that was too likely.

"He won't be beating on her anymore, at least. She died last night. We just picked him up. He's just waiting for a PD to come talk to him. We're overbooked in the holding cells so we left him out here, figured everybody knows him, he ain't going anywhere."

Erin felt sickened listening to him. There was too much cruelty in the world.

"What's a PD?" she asked, hoping to change the subject.

"PD? Oh yeah, it's a public defender. People like Stanley out there can't afford a real lawyer, so they have to take their chances with the ones the state coughs up. He'll have about fifteen minutes before he goes to court, if history repeats itself. Just about all he needs." Erin thought he looked awful blasé about the whole thing. She told him so.

"Yeah, I guess you're right. I've been around here a long time, and after awhile you get blind to most of the things that go on. Now somebody like him, he's not a killer, not really. He just got frustrated, had a few drinks and then the situation got out of control. Just lucky he didn't have a gun, or this might have gotten really ugly when the cops showed up." He paused and looked a little uncomfortable, like he wasn't accustomed to speaking like this to a citizen. He went on. "The PD will go over the case, plead it out in court, and Stanley will serve about three years, more or less. It's not like he's gonna run out and start smacking people again or anything like that. Now the situation we got, you and me, is a whole world away from that."

Erin asked how, although she could see the differences pretty clearly.

He waited a long time before speaking. He opened the folder on the desk and flipped through the pages, pausing on the pictures of the man in the hospital bed. Glancing at Erin and back again to the photos he took one out and handed it to her. Her face went white and he could tell she was about to cry.

"Anybody who could do that, inflict that sort of pain to someone he doesn't know is just off the scale. I think you were right, I think this was the guy from the food court."

She choked out a response. Even with the picture turned face down on the scarred table, in her mind she could see the damage. "You do? Why?"

"I don't know, really. And what I think is not something that I could ever prove, or even feel comfortable saying out loud. Certainly not out there." He nodded toward the squad room beyond the glass and then shook his head. "Like I said, I've been around here along time, and I was raised in a cop family. My grandfather was a Pinkerton Op, buddies with Dashiell Hammett. You know Hammett, the guy who wrote *The Maltese Falcon*?"

"Yes. I'm just a little surprised that you do." Erin replied, instantly regretting it.

He laughed. "That's okay, I guess cops don't strike people as big readers. Most of the time you'd be right. Like I was saying, my grandfather was a cop, my dad was a cop, too, up in Chicago. So when I hear about people like Adam I'm not just talking out of my hat. He's like nothing I've ever seen before, and that scares me. If a person can make a roomful of witnesses see different things, then all the rules go out the window. It was luck that a kid saw him in the mall bathroom. His description matches up for the most part with yours."

She stopped him, amazed.

"Someone else saw him? Are you sure?" She had never known this before, and it made the feelings she had concerning who he was a little easier to deal with.

"I didn't believe him until you started telling us what you remembered the other day, but once you did it all works out. We sent out the pictures that you did with the sketch artist to about three hundred police stations around the country. Maybe we'll get lucky."

"What do think your chances are?" She asked.

"Slim to none." He sighed. "Of course, I'd rather be lucky than good. Maybe somebody saw him, could recognize him. Give it awhile."

The idea of Adam walking around loose frightened her.

"So what do you think makes him more dangerous than the other people you have in here?"

"It's not just him, I don't think. That's what scares me. A person like that could be a harbinger of things to come. Just seems like open season out there now, you know?" She nodded and he went on. "Everyday we pick bodies off the street like it was the plague all over again. When we catch somebody the chances of us getting a conviction are pretty slim, and if he does take the rap then we can bet on seeing him back again in a few years. So if a person can do shit like this and walk away from it without anyone even seeing him, well, it makes our job impossible instead of just improbable. I don't mind saying that I've been thinking of packing it in, take a cushy little security job and just nap out my remaining years until retirement. Then I can move to Miami and read about German tourists getting shot on the freeway." When he spoke Erin could tell that he wasn't really looking at her, not even exactly talking to her. He seemed to be talking to himself. He noticed and apologized.

"Sorry about that. I don't have an reason to be talking like that around you."

"That's all right. Is it really that bad? I mean, what can you do?" Hearing this sort of speech coming from a cop didn't exactly calm Erin's fears about Adam walking around beyond these walls.

"What can we do? Practically nothing, if you want to know the truth. Right now the criminal has most of the advantage in a situation. The only thing that is going to make a difference is tougher law, sort of even it out on the side of the cops."

She didn't agree. Even though she considered herself pretty neutral when it came to politics, one of the things she did feel was that there were already too many laws. If only they were enforced perhaps the situation would change. She told him so.

"I guess I didn't explain it right. I'm not talking about stiffer penalties." He leaned closer to her over the desk, and spoke in a lower, sort of conspiratorial manner. "I wouldn't admit out there, but I'm against the death penalty." She looked surprised.

"Why?" She figured all cops were in favor of letting the criminal fry.

"Because it doesn't work, far as I can tell. We got thousands of people sitting in death rows all around the country who know that the only reason they are there is because they are black and poor, and most likely they will die of natural causes before the sentence ever gets carried out. No, what I'm talking about is more along the lines of martial law. Curfews, gun control, the whole bit. Make it real plain who is the good guy and who isn't." Even though his voice had stayed even throughout Erin could tell this was something he felt strongly about.

"Isn't that getting away from the reason this country was made?"

"Look around, Erin! Does this place look anything like what we started with? No, this country is a war zone. I've seen little kids, six, seven years old carrying guns. I've watched mothers sell crack out of their baby's diapers and skinheads kick an old black man to death just for being in the wrong place collecting cans! And people like your buddy Adam are just the next in a long line of crap that we've been dealing with for years." He leaned back in the chair and rubbed his eyes, exhausted. He hadn't slept much since this whole thing started, and he needed a break. He looked over at the woman sitting across from him. He wondered what she was thinking.

"Can I ask you something?" His voice was gentler now.

"Yes, that's why I'm here, isn't it?" Erin responded.

He ignored the jab, if that was what it was.

"No, I was just wondering why you didn't stop him? Why did you tell him where to find Tyler, what he looked like? I mean, you seem to be a pretty normal lady, not like Stanley out there. I'm just curious."

Erin sat for a moment, wondering how to vocalize the emotions she had lived with since this had started. When she spoke it was from somewhere in her that she didn't encounter very often, maybe never before.

"Because he deserved it." She said, tears welling up in her eyes.

CHAPTER 16

Hunches. Gut feelings. Theories. When that's all that's left in a case, you pack it in. Nelson knew that to be one school. Equally true was the idea that once you eliminated everything else what was left was the answer, even if it seemed impossible. Since he wasn't ready to call it quits yet, he went with the latter. It had worked before.

He thought about this as he sat behind his house, smelling the honeysuckle that grew along the rocky banks of the creek. In some places the delicate plant would appear out of a seemingly solid face of stone, adapting to the surroundings in a desire to bloom and grow. In others it grew over, under and around an existing bush, until the original plant suffocated and died.

The longer he stared at the little white blossoms the clearer he became. He had been right when he spoke to Erin that morning, even though at the time he had just been letting off steam. This person, this Adam, was different. Different and new. New meant dangerous. If what he thought was true, if Adam could change his appearance on command, make people see what he wanted them to see, then it was like the honeysuckle adapting to the world around it in the quest to survive.

He heard a car pull into his driveway. He rose to check it out and met Philip rounding the house.

"Thought I'd find you out here when you didn't answer the phone," his partner said.

"When did you call?"

"Just a second ago, from the car." Banks laughed at the idea. He wasn't real thrilled with the future, what he had seen of it.

"So what's up?" he asked, wondering why Maxwell would come by. "Something going on downtown?"

"No, nothing that can't wait. I just noticed that you seem a bit down lately, wondered if there was something I could do."

Nelson was taken aback for a moment by the statement. He guessed that he and Philip were friends, since they worked together everyday, but he wasn't the type to offer like that, and Nelson wasn't the sort to go looking. Still, it might be good to run some of the things he had been pondering past Maxwell. If they didn't come up with any better ideas then he would continue on by himself.

"Philip, how long have you been a cop?"

"About fifteen years. Why?"

"I've been doing it for almost twenty-five, and I've never felt as useless as I do now. When I saw that man in the hospital something just went out of me. I have these ideas, crazy ideas."

"Like what? Anything's better than nothing, which is what we got now, right?" Maxwell reached down and pulled a beer from the ones Nelson had left to cool in the slow moving creek and twisted off the cap. He drank and waited for Nelson to speak.

"Doesn't it seem like this town, hell, the world is just getting crazy? You realize we had twenty-three murders in the last month, and that's all single shootings? And that thing at the airport, I don't know, I just feel our boy is in on it."

Maxwell looked up in surprise and righted his beer on the ground before he knocked it over.

"Why? What's the connection?"

"None, and that's the whole thing. We know that Adam was in town, or could have been. He's a man that kills on the command of others, and so far nobody has stepped forward to take credit for it, like usually happens. And somehow it just feels the same." He paused to gather words. "Overkill. The man in the mall, he could have been taken out in a hundred places a lot more private and safer, but instead he does it in the middle of a crowd of people. Like he was sure he wouldn't get caught. Then the guy in the hospital, I mean really! A simple beating would have had the same effect. Instead he takes his time and ruins that guy's life. So naturally the bomb thing just makes me think of him. Overkill."

"Yeah, three hundred plus of overkill. I think I see what you're saying. So how do we catch him?"

"I think that Erin is our link. She was able to locate him the last time, maybe she could do it again."

"Would she?"

"I think so. I mean, it's just a hunch but we don't have anything else, do we?"

Philip shook his head no.

"How is she going to do it, I mean we tried the number on that card ourselves. It was disconnected, remember?"

"This sounds nuts, but follow me. I think if she uses that number, calls him up, it will ring."

To Nelson's relief his partner didn't look at him like he was nuts. He felt nuts, so Philip must be acting polite.

"What will we do if he answers?"

"Hope to get him interested enough to see her again, for starters."

"Then what? I don't think we are gonna be able to get a conviction on this guy, do you? He doesn't strike me as the confessing type."

Nelson looked at the honeysuckle again, climbing over the rocks.

"Who said I would give him the chance?"

CHAPTER 17

Nelson and Philip sat in Erin Welch's living room. On the coffee table between them sat the card that Adam had given her in the bar. It had taken Nelson a few days to convince Erin to do this, and more still to wait until her husband Ralph had been out of town. Why that was part of the deal he didn't know, and he didn't understand why she hadn't told him about the incident. She had her reasons, he imagined.

Maxwell knelt under a table, attaching a tape recorder to the phone, in order to record both sides of the conversation, if one occurred. Nelson was of course hoping that it would, but he didn't really think the chances were good. Philip stood up and nodded to him that he was ready. Nelson looked at Erin and he could tell she was nervous. The idea of calling forced her to think about all that occurred, and that must be hard. Still, she knew she had to do something, or the idea of him being out there was always going to haunt her.

"What should I say?" She was afraid that if he answered the phone she would freeze up, or let on that there was someone with her. She didn't want to think about him coming for her, as she knew he would if he felt cornered.

"Just get him talking, set up a meeting. Tell him you have something you want done. Can you do that?" Nelson sounded patient.

"Okay." She picked up the phone and started to dial. Banks put on the headset from the recorder, so he could hear what was being said, if anything. Erin began to dial. He could see the card shaking in her hand, and she paused before punching the last number. He nodded to her, and she pushed the key. For a moment the faint hum of static filled the earpiece. When the sound of the phone ringing burst through it seemed louder than it should, probably because it was unexpected. Nelson gave the thumbs-up sign to Philip and the three in the room seemed to let out the breath that they were holding.

The phone rang again, and a third time. When a voice interrupted Erin almost dropped the phone.

"Hello?" The sound was flat, emotionless in Nelson's ears.

"Adam, this is Erin."

"How are you, Erin? Had any trouble with Tyler since the last time we spoke?"

"Of course not!" the voice in her head screamed, "he's still in the hospital, you crazy fucker." Erin forced herself to calm down before she spoke.

"No, not a sound. Thank you." Was there more to say? Erin stayed quiet, waiting for him to speak.

"Is there something else I can do for you Erin?"

"Yes ... I think so."

"What's that?" The voice on the phone didn't match up with what Nelson had pictured in his mind, although what that was he couldn't say. He had expected it to sound different. He had imagined that he would have gotten from it a sense of a man unbalanced. Instead, it sounded like a man having a conversation with a friend, just chatting about any old thing. Not one planning a killing.

"Go on, Erin. You can tell me."

"It's my husband, Ralph."

"What do you want me to do? You can tell me. Trust me, it gets easier the more you do it." The voice had a chuckle in it, and Erin dropped her hand to her lap, covering the phone with her palm. She looked at Maxwell and pointed to the bar in the corner. "Get me a drink!" He went to the bar and poured a few inches of scotch into a glass, after unwrapping it from the paper it was packed in. She gulped it down and put the phone back to her ear.

"Sorry. I needed to get a drink." The liquor had burned her throat but she felt better. "I want you to kill him." Nelson and Philip locked eyes, both wondering how much of this was improvisation, and how much was real.

Erin felt horrible as soon as the words had left her mouth. Could he tell she was lying? Was she lying?

"Okay, fine. I'll need some details from you."

Erin's eyes showed the panic she felt and she looked up at Nelson. He wrote the word "meeting" on a pad of paper on the table and she nodded, afraid. She didn't want to see him again, ever.

"Like what?"

"A picture, where he works, that sort of thing."

"Don't you even want to know why?" Erin asked.

"Does it really matter? If you want this done, then show up at the pool at Piedmont Park tomorrow at noon. If not, then I'll see you around." The phone clicked dead. Erin dropped her end down and Maxwell began working with the tape deck, taking the headphones from Nelson and listening to the whole conversation, as Nelson had.

Erin sat on the couch, looking stunned.

"You did good. After tomorrow, all this will be over," Nelson said to the woman, and went on to explain the details to her.

Leaving the house and driving away both men wondered if it would really be over after tomorrow. They drove back to the station, absorbed in the details of what they had to do before noon tomorrow. Maxwell had convinced Nelson, after much discussion, to let this be a police action. And in the end, what had finally won him over was the mention of his dad, and how he had instilled in him the notions of law and order and justice. He thought about this as they left the tree-covered neighborhood and turned on to the busy street heading back to the station. Absorbed in his thoughts he never noticed the gray sedan move past them.

CHAPTER 18

Like Nelson, Adam shared a basic dislike of the changes of the future, but he had to admit that cell phones came in handy. Most people imagined that when they called a phone number it rang in a room somewhere, somewhere stationary and at least semi-permanent. With a phone like this, he had realized years ago, a person could roam around the world and no one would ever know that they weren't talking to a man in a room. The phone had been cheap, and for a few hundred dollars more he had found a young computer whiz to tap into the phone company database and change the makeup of the number assigned to the phone. Now, when the number was dialed the phone company computers checked the area code and prefix of the number. If it was one of the ones on a list that Adam had supplied, then the phone rang. If not, the call was blocked, and sounded to the caller as if it had never rung. A trace of the number would lead nowhere, since Adam's friend had wiped it from the phone listings. Technology could be useful, Adam admitted.

He watched the two men in the dark blue car pass by him, and he knew they were cops because he recognized the older one from the mall. He pounded his hand on the steering wheel in frustration. He was getting old, old and careless. He had lingered too long in Atlanta, and hadn't paid attention to the signs around him.

He was only in his mid-thirties, but the way he had lived his life had made him old before his time. He should have left after the airport, stolen a car and just driven back to New Orleans. If he had he would have made it in time for the jazz festival, one of the few treats to living in a city as god-forsaken as the Big Easy. Why he stuck around Atlanta he didn't really know. Now that he had, he knew that he would have to get rid of the pair of cops, or spend the next few years looking over his back. He knew that this too was a sign of his failings, his sense of sharpness having dulled over the years. He had done jobs all over the world, hundreds he supposed, although he never had the time to stop and count. He had left each one without a trace. He had money back in New Orleans, and if he got there it would be enough for him to retire from the business. The prospect of quitting didn't bother him, in fact it was sort of appealing, although he didn't really know what he would do with his time.

What had the old man done, all those years ago? Adam remembered a quick meeting once, the man on the edge of death, just months after he had given it all up, when he passed on the last of his knowledge to Adam. They had spoken for a bit, but the old man hadn't wanted him around, his purpose in life completed, and Adam had left. He found out later that the man had died a few weeks after that. He imagined that the same would happen to him. The thought didn't really bother him.

Still he had the problem here to take care of. He needed somebody with him, to act as eyes around the park. He picked up the phone and punched in a number. It rang and then a sleepy voice answered.

"Yeah, go ahead." Adam cringed at the rudeness.

"That's no way to answer a phone, Robert." Adam had made contact with the boy a few weeks ago, following him as he had the woman from the mall. The young man had seen him in the bathroom that day, and Adam had initially thought he would have to kill him, to clear up loose ends. After talking to him he decided against it, even though he found the man to be rather unbalanced, most likely from the sweet smoke of the drug he inhaled. He was able to tell right off the bat that Morris had no intention of talking to the police any more than he already had, and that he might be helpful in the future. The boy was strong, and didn't seem to have any problems with some of the things Adam had asked him to do. He knew the boy had killed, although as of yet Adam hadn't asked him to. In a perverse way he saw himself as a catcher in the rye, as from the book. Of course, not everyone would agree with that, Adam chuckled to himself.

"What the hell, you woke me up." Robert sounded more alert now, and Adam could hear the rasp of a match as he lit a cigarette.

"I need your help tomorrow. You free?"

"Sure man, what's up?"

"Just need you to cover my back, check out an area for me. Not very long."

"Cool. Like what does it pay?"

"Good, you're learning." Already the boy had a sense of worth, the same that he had learned when he was that age.

"I'll make it worth your while. Just meet me at the Majestic Diner around eight tonight, okay? You know the place?"

"Sure, down on Ponce. No problem. Do I need to bring anything, a gun or something?" Adam stared at the phone. For all its advantages it still had one major drawback that it worked off radio waves. Anyone nearby with a strong receiver could pick up the conversation.

"Remember what I told you, about phones?" Good instincts on this kid, but it would take Adam awhile to hammer home the finer points.

"Yeah, whatever. See you tonight." The boy hung up and Adam set the phone down. As he drove down the streets that led out of Erin's neighborhood he switched on the radio, letting the music wash over him. Yes, it was time to retire, let the next generation take his place. When he and the old man had traveled together he had wondered aloud how many people there had been like him, ones with the special talents he had.

"Not many. And after you, no one."

Adam had been confused. All along the old man had tried to make him understand that he was nothing more than a part of a longer process, one that would some day move the world to its dying days. So how could he be the last?

"The last with such a trait, that's all I mean. After you the numbers of people who are like us will continue to double, and double again. They will be so many of them that they won't have a need for special gifts, like you and me. They'll just do what comes naturally, and that will be enough."

It had taken years for Adam to understand. But these days, looking around the streets, he knew what the old man had meant.

CHAPTER 19

Adam waited atop the concrete building that sat next to the pool. It was low with a ladder built into the side. He had been here all morning, since just after sun-up, hidden by a large air conditioning unit. Joggers had run by, trying to get in their distance before the cloudless sky baked the people below. Robert was down the hill, on a bench at the edge of a path leading up to this point. Both had radios, and Adam depressed the talk button, checking in with Morris.

"You still down there?"

"Yeah, but man, this is boring as shit. How much longer am I gonna have to sit out here? It's starting to get hot."

"You have to learn to wait." He looked at his watch. A quarter to noon. "Just a little while longer. You see the cop?" Adam was relying on the boy recognizing the detective that had questioned him before.

"No." Robert lifted his head up from the newspaper he was supposed to look like he was reading and glanced around the area again. Just a few people further down the hill, playing Frisbee with a dog, two guys in shorts.

"Stay alert. If you see him, let me know."

"You want me to follow him, give you a hand?"

"No, don't want to take a chance on him seeing you and remembering you from the police station."

"Man, that was awhile ago. I doubt the guy would remember me now," he said with a scoffing tone.

"Never underestimate your opponent. It might save your life." Adam switched off the radio and raised his head over the rusted edge of the air conditioning unit. He could see to Piedmont Road, which rimmed the edge of the park. He waited and watched, flipping down the sunglasses on his head so he wouldn't have to squint. More people were starting into the park now, in two's and three's, some with kids, others with dogs on long leashes. He could hear the bark of one, carrying over the grass.

It reminded him of the dogs he had killed when he was a boy. That was what caught the attention of the old man, although Adam never learned how he found out about it. When he left home it had been to go with the man up to the Green River in Washington. The three-day car trip had been a learning experience for him. Along the way they had stopped to pick up a friend of the old man, a handsome younger man who seemed nervous, bundled up in two or three layers of clothes. They had waited while the man had stolen a car, a VW, and driven off into the night. Adam had asked the old man who the rider had been. He told him not to worry, you'll hear his name again. He was right. Years later he had followed the trial of Ted Bundy on the news, and noticed after that when they executed him in Florida. He wondered if the same fate awaited him, and he knew if he were ever caught it would be because he screwed up, not because some cop got smart.

It was five after twelve when Adam saw Erin coming up from the street. He turned the radio back on and hit scan. He watched as the red lights jumped from number to number, not settling on anything. The police weren't using radios. He pushed the transmit button and called to Robert.

"See anything?"

"Nah, just those old dudes playing Frisbee."

"Anybody else?" Adam asked.

"No."

"Okay, get up and come around the other side of the pool, let me know if you see anything." Adam turned the volume low on the radio and stuck it in his pocket. Standing up he moved down the ladder and started across the field toward Erin. She was wearing shorts, with a sleeveless top. She didn't have a purse, and her hands were empty. This was a trap. She hadn't brought anything with her like he had asked. He changed his course and headed for a grove of dogwood trees clustered around the path that snaked through the park. She hadn't seen him.

He lifted the radio to his mouth and spoke low. "It's off. Get out of the park." The radio stayed silent after he spoke. Idiot had turned it off. He looked around, trying to see Robert past the tree line. No sign of him anywhere. He looked back to Erin and saw her sitting under a tree, looking at the pool. No one was around her, but that didn't mean there weren't cops in the tree line around the grassy field.

This was something he had expected, the call from Erin being a trick to get him into the open. That's why he had brought Robert along, to give him an extra pair of eyes. Of course that all went for nothing if the fool didn't keep the radio on. He looked back in the direction where Morris had been heading. Still no sign of him. Adam began walking out of the cover of the trees and onto the path, speeding up slightly to get behind a group of blacks carrying folding chairs and a small grill. He turned and looked for Robert again, before he left. Let the kid get out himself. All he could see was an older man in shorts, holding a Frisbee in one hand.

And a radio in the other.

CHAPTER 20

If you can't be good, be lucky. And Nelson knew that when he saw that Morris kid sitting on a bench, reading a newspaper, that luck had come his way. First off, there was a connection between Adam and this boy Robert, at least in Nelson's mind, and second, from what he had gathered from his questioning of the boy he wasn't the type to sit down and read a newspaper. So he was up to something, and as he watched him talk on the radio he figured it out.

After confronting him, he listened to the radio and waited and heard Adam describe the trap. It had taken only a second of pressure on the boy's hand before he said where Adam had hidden himself.

Nelson knew if he ran up the hill he would give himself away. He felt damn foolish as it was, standing in shorts and a Polo shirt, throwing a Frisbee to a dog. He had backup cops hidden around the park, but he still felt vulnerable without a gun or a radio. He had been hoping to get close enough to Adam to surprise him, and he couldn't have done that dressed like a cop. Of course that was all blown now. Now he had to find him, before Adam blended in with the crowd in the park and disappeared.

He looked at the pool and the building beside it but could see nothing. He walked slowly up the hill, nearing a stand of trees. The white petals of the dogwoods swayed slightly in the wind, but they hid no one in their midst. He walked around them, his eyes moving back and forth from area to area. A typical weekend crowd at the park. Couples hand in hand, lying under the trees, parents with yelling children running down the hills. Up ahead on a path was a black family, arms laden with the makings of a picnic. Father, son, wife and two daughters, all weighed down with plastic chairs, grills and armloads of food. He stopped and looked up the slow slope of the hill leading into the park. He could see Erin, leaning against a tree, the branches of the oak starting thirty or forty feet above her head. She sat staring at the pool, not moving.

He thought of going to her, to protect her if Adam made a grab for her, although he thought that unlikely. He was probably long gone by now, swallowed up in the city that surrounded the park. He had been smart when he picked this place, using the sort of logic that Nelson had expected. Higher on the hill, between Erin and the road he caught sight of Maxwell, arms crossed, looking out over the park, his eyes always coming back to Erin. He could keep an eye on her, while he looked around to see if Adam was still in the area.

He turned and looked back the way he had come, to see if Adam had waited as Nelson had walked by, and was trying to leave. How would he know him if he saw him? Erin had given him a description, as had Morris, but he wouldn't know until the time came if they had been accurate enough.

He moved his eyes back over the park. The kid's yells had faded as they had reached the end of the hill, and the lovers under the tree had progressed from hand holding to embracing. A lot better way to spend a Saturday than his, chasing a madman who seemed to be a ghost. Moving into the middle of the path, he watched the backs of the family continue on to find a good spot for their picnic. The father in front, a head taller than his family, although his sons came close.

Sons.

Nelson began moving toward them, not fast enough to make a sound, at the same trying to make sure that he was remembering the makeup of the group correctly from before. Mother, father, two daughters and one teenage boy. One. The person bringing up the rear of the party would look like all the others, except to the family themselves, and he was far enough back that they would just take him for another face in the crowd. As yet the man hadn't turned around, so Nelson felt safe. Dangling from a pocket was the same sort of cord that Nelson could see on the radio he had taken from Morris.

This son of a bitch can really do it. All those people in the mall had been right. Those coeds in Florida too, and who knows how many others. He couldn't stop to ponder now, and it took all he had not to rush Adam and jump him, but the road was winding downhill, and if his momentum carried him past the man he would end up in a pile of angry people. So he kept a steady pace until he was arm's length from him.

He reached out and grabbed Adam's elbow. He felt powerful muscles tense, but the man stopped walking and made no attempt to escape.

"So, what is this?"

Nelson studied the face in front of him. How it had changed, he hadn't been able to see, even though his eyes had never stopped looking at him. The man was about Nelson's height, less heavy, but looked as if he was strong. His face was smooth, with no lines or marks. He seemed to be in his mid-thirties, but it was hard to tell. If it weren't for the straight black hair, he would have looked like any of a hundred people you see everyday and don't notice a bit.

"Your name Adam Winter?"

"Has been. What's yours?"

"Nelson Banks. I want you to come with me, answer a few questions."

"A little under prepared, aren't we? I mean, no gun, no handcuffs?" Adam spoke with a mocking tone.

"Well, my partner, he looks better in this stuff than I do. You'll meet him in a minute. Come on." Nelson kept the pressure on the man's arm, and led him up the path. He motioned to Philip. Soon, uniformed police clogged the path, called out on Maxwell's signal.

"Is Erin still here? I want to tell her she has been very brave."

"She knew we had her covered. She wasn't in any danger." Nelson replied, annoyed by the man's conversational tone.

"I'm not talking about today."

CHAPTER 21

Adam remained silent as the uniformed cops took him from Nelson and pushed him into a car. He looked contained enough, with his hands cuffed behind his back and two uniformed cops in the car with him, but Nelson knew that the first chance Adam saw he would bolt, and leave them empty-handed. He waved down the car and it slowed to a stop beside him.

"I'm gonna ride this one down with you." He started to get into the back of the car with Adam.

"Whatever you say." The driver said.

The cop hit the siren and lights to clear a way out of the park, but other than that the ride was silent. Nelson looked at his prisoner. He was staring out the window, looking calm. He wanted to ask him questions; for there were things he couldn't understand.

"How do you do that change thing?" Nelson asked. Adam was quiet, and Nelson wondered if he was ignoring him, or if he hadn't heard the question.

"I don't," he answered after a few moments. "People see what they want to see, what they perceive life to be. I'm just a mirror. I don't really exist to them. I just give them a suggestion, a form to attach all their notions and fears on. How it actually happens, I don't really know. I've always been able to do it. Sometimes it's harder than others."

"Like today?"

"Yeah, I was a little distracted today." Adam smiled after he spoke. "What happened to Robert?"

"We took him downtown, same place we're taking you. Why, you afraid of what he might tell us?"

"He doesn't know enough to tell, believe me. I just wondered, that's all." Adam went back to looking out the window.

"Is he like you? I mean, does he change?" The notion scared Banks, imagining a whole legion of people like Adam wandering around.

"No, not that I'm aware of. He's just somebody I met who I thought would come in handy. He doesn't need anything like that. He's a child of the times, and that's enough."

Nelson had no idea what the man was talking about, but people like this, hardcore types, never made any sense. And now that he had him, Nelson felt as tired as he ever had. He still wanted to know more, so he blinked his eyes and stared at Adam, sitting quietly, looking out the car window.

"Are you a hit man, or what? Or do you just do this for kicks?"

Adam looked at Nelson. His gaze was powerful, his face calm. Smug bastard, Banks thought.

"I guess you could say I'm like a hit man, I mean I don't do the things I do for fun. I'm not like your Manson or Gacy." Nelson shuddered at the mention of the man's name. "Let me ask you something. Why do you do the things you do, like chasing someone like me? Doesn't it get frustrating, all this evil around you, and you and the other police so few, so powerless? What makes you go on?" Adam said.

"Somebody has to. It's in my blood. I was raised to be a cop, my whole family was cops. I don't know anything else."

Adam smiled as he spoke, the sight scaring Nelson. "Neither do I."

"We're here. Where do you want him?" one of the uniforms from the front said.

"Get him processed, then throw him in a cell. By himself, you understand?" Nelson didn't want to take a chance on someone mistaking Adam for somebody else. "I want you two to walk him personally through the whole thing. Make sure he doesn't get out of your eyesight, right?"

"What, you think he's going to fly away?" The cops laughed.

"Just watch him, all right?"

Philip was already at his desk, assembling the different case files. He looked up as Nelson sat down.

"He say anything?"

"Hell no. Course I don't expect he will. You don't last long in that sort of an environment if you have a loose mouth." Nelson wondered just how long Adam had been killing. He wondered if he would ever find out.

"So you ready to do a line-up? I got Erin downstairs, ready to go."

"How's she doing?" Nelson worried about her, about what this had done to her life, how it would define what she did from now on.

"She's holding up, I guess. I think she just wants to get it over with. Like we all do."

"Ain't that the truth."

Philip opened a file and looked at it.

"You think we should send his picture down to Williams? Maybe somebody from the campus could ID him."

"Sure, but that's a long shot. What's the deal on Morris? He gonna sit in on the lineup?"

"I don't think so. He's already got a lawyer on the horn, and he hasn't spoken much since we booked him. Not a real outgoing kid."

"Well, run it by him again. Who knows, maybe he'll feel like cooperating when we explain it to him." Nelson got up and poured some water in a cup and then started digging around in his desk, looking for aspirin.

"Here, take some of mine." Maxwell threw a bottle over and Nelson gulped three tablets down with the water.

"Thanks. I feel like shit."

"Don't look so good either. Why don't you go home, crash out for awhile? Its just paperwork for the time being. We can question him in the morning."

"No, I want to talk to him tonight, run him through a lineup. I don't want to take a chance on him shaking out of here. We've gone this far, I'd hate to lose him now." He stopped talking for a second and looked down at the floor, and then slowly looked up at his partner.

"Let me ask you something."

"Shoot."

"When I was telling you all this stuff, did you believe me?"

"Not really. But I trust your instincts, so I decided to wait it out, see if anything happened. I don't know why, but I figured you've been around here a lot longer than I have, I guess."

"Well, thanks. Tell you the truth, I don't really believe it myself. I think this is the last one." Maxwell started to speak in protest, but Nelson shut him off. "No, really. It's not just this case, although I don't think I want to go through something like this again. Too old. No, it's just that I don't like the way people look at me when I tell them I'm a cop. You ever get that?"

Philip nodded. "My wife's folks think I'm some sort of fascist. They're all the time trying to bait me into arguments about some shit they saw on the TV or read in the paper. I know what you mean, but that's just part of the job. You get used to it. People might not want you around when everything's going good, but let them hear a strange sound in the dark of night and what do they do? Call a cop."

"No, they get a gun out of the bedside table and shoot their husband coming back from the bathroom. Then they call the cops."

"I guess you're right, sometimes. So why's this stuff just starting to get to you now?" Philip sat waiting for an answer, tapping a pencil against his fingers to pass the time.

Nelson didn't really have a reason. He thought about his dad, sitting alone in the house in Chicago, tormented by the visions he had gotten from Gacy. Nelson didn't want to end up like that, the life sucked out of him by the job.

"I don't know. Hell, I'm just beat. Let's go down and see our boy. Maybe we'll get lucky." As he stood and pulled on his coat, he knew that as a cop, the luckiest he could get would be for Adam to tell all. As a man, however, he hoped that didn't happen.

CHAPTER 22

It took most of the afternoon to arrange the line-up. Finally, as the light from the day was beginning to fade away from the windows of the station, they brought Erin into a small room with just a desk, a few chairs and a large window. Erin knew in her head that it was one-way glass, but it still frightened her.

"Do you understand what's going to happen?" Nelson handed her a cup of water as he spoke.

"Yes. Are you sure he can't see us?" Her hands shook as she sipped the water. She noticed and kept them in her lap after setting the cup down.

"No, he can't see in, only we can see out. But he knows who is in here. He knows that the thing today in the park was a setup." Nelson didn't want to scare her off, but she must have figured this out already.

"I understand. What are his chances of getting out?"

"You mean legally?"

"Yes."

"None, as it stands now. He hasn't requested a lawyer, so after you ID him we'll take him upstairs and set up an arraignment. He'll be charged with murder one, conspiracy to commit murder, and whatever else we can get out of him. No judge is going to set bail, not with him being a flight risk. Adam's not the kind of guy that would let us watch him run on CNN." Nelson didn't venture to answer the other part of her question. He didn't want to think about Adam's chances of escape. The lights went on in the room past the window, and six men began filing in. All were about Adam's height and weight, and he was next to last in line. A voice told the men to turn one way and then another, and finally to face the glass.

Erin spoke as soon as the men stood still.

"He's number five, the next to last one." She felt relieved that she could do this.

"Right." Nelson stepped to the wall and pressed a button. "Take 'em back. We're all done in here." A cop led the men out. As he passed the window Adam turned and looked at it. Erin could swear he could see her. Philip opened the door and looked down the hall, waiting until it was clear. He told Nelson okay and they left the room. In the hallway Erin stopped the two and asked what came next.

"Well, like Nelson said, he's going to be arraigned in the morning and then we start gathering information to give to the D.A. We won't need you until later, if they decide to use you at the trial. That's gonna be a while from now, don't ya think, Nelson?"

"Most likely. Could be we won't need you at all. We have the knife from the mall, and maybe his fingerprints will match the ones we got off of it. We'll wait and see." Banks started walking down the hall, taking Erin lightly by the arm. "I'll walk you to your car."

"Thank you."

Philip headed the other way, toward the stairs, ready to start the endless paperwork they faced.

"See ya in a little while, okay?" Nelson called to him. They reached the door leading to the parking lots and Erin pointed out her car. They walked in silence, and Nelson listened to the sounds of the city go on around them, the hiss of bus brakes, the thump of a car stereo playing too loud. Damn, he hated that rap shit.

"You going to be all right?" Erin could hear the concern in his voice.

"I don't know. I just want to forget all this ever happened. I want to thank you for not having me arrested, as you could have. I guess I owe you something."

"If you help us get this guy, and you have, then I think you and I will be even. If you need to talk, give me a call. I'll try to keep you out of this as much as I can, okay?"

She opened her door and got into the car.

"Too late for that, isn't it?"

CHAPTER 23

Bars made up three of the four walls of the cell; the fourth was brick, spotted here and there by graffiti. Adam sat and watched the room outside the bars go about its business. The two police who had driven him in were seated in front of him at a desk, talking to each other and occasionally glancing over at Adam. He hadn't moved since they set him down on the stainless steel bench in the holding cell, and neither man could understand the insistence of Banks that they keep an eye on him. The guy seemed harmless enough, even though he was facing arraignment on murder charges. Still, if they were going to collect overtime for watching a guy sit in a cell, so be it.

Adam focused hard on the last few hours. He knew from the moment he heard Erin's voice on the phone that it could be a trap. Why didn't he walk away? A few years ago he would have trusted his instincts and never shown up at the park. He knew that a large measure of it was pride, to test whether his abilities still outmatched those of his adversary. It was a foolish play, one that he knew he could lose. He had resisted all these years the impulse to do things for his reasons, to commit crimes on his own volition, to mix with the people he worked for. Now, his drive to prove to himself that he still commanded the power he had used for so long had ended with him in a twelve-by- ten cell, being watched like a colicky baby by two rookie cops. He felt anger begin to grow inside, and he couldn't let it show. At the moment he was only handcuffed, easily enough removed. As long as he sat quietly, there would be no need for leg irons or a waist chain. Now, he would wait. Wait and listen.

One floor down, in the basement of the station, Robert Morris sat on a bench, surrounded by crack heads and drunks. His lawyer had rushed by the holding tank hours ago, and he hadn't seen him since. He sat far away from his nearest bench mate, an older man who had passed out soon after they had threw him in the room. He smelled of urine, and was missing a shoe. As he slept off the effects of cheap wine sour breath hissed out of his mouth as though from a slowly leaking tire.

Everyone in the room except the sleeper looked up as keys struck the door. It slid back and a large, wild-haired teenager stumbled in, face contorted, an oath cut off as the door clanged shut, leaving him without an audience. Robert recognized him from one of the clubs around town.

"Robert, my man! What the fuck brings you in here?" The man spoke as he slid down the wall next to Robert, stretching his legs out across the floor.

"Ah, nothin' man. Just helping a dude out in the park, and the man picked me up. What about you?" Robert didn't really care, but you end up talking to people in places like this that you most likely would pass by on the street.

"Shoplifting, can you fuckin' believe it? Leaving Buddy's gas station, like I always do, was going down to Little Five Points, check out the scene, and this fucking car slams on its brakes right when I started to cross the road! Two quart bottles of Mickeys fall out of my shirt, and naturally, the prick that almost ran me down was a cop! Of course by that time the little Korean asshole who runs the place comes out yip yip yippin' that I stole some beer, and here I am. What a bitch."

Robert laughed. He remembered the first time he had seen this guy, in a parking lot across from the Star Bar, the jerk had almost lit his Fugazi shirt on fire smoking rock. Hang around people like that you see pretty quickly why they call it dope.

The man leaned over to Robert and spoke softly.

"You holding?" The guy looked pretty eager.

"In a police station?" Guy's a dead zone upstairs.

"Yeah, all right, chill. I'll make do with what I got." Robert watched as the man reached down into a worn boot and pulled out a rag. Out of the other boot he pulled a can of lighter fluid, and squirted it over the dirty cloth and held it to his face. After about thirty seconds his hand began to flutter and then fell into his lap. His chin dropped down to his chest, and Robert watched as his eyes sank shut momentarily.

Robert looked around the cell, seeing if anyone had noticed. Everyone was busy looking out the small window set in the door or trying to sleep. You don't make a lot of eye contact in situations like these, unless you want to start trouble. He had been in a tank like this once when a fight had flared up between two men arguing over a book of matches. He remembered that the doors to the cell hadn't opened until one of the men lay on the floor and the other had slumped against the wall, spent, and the room had returned to quiet. Whatever started in here was going to end in here, he had learned from a safe distance. That's just where he would stay.

Suddenly the man next to him sat up to a crouch and shook his head.

"Sweet! Fuckin' A that feels excellent!" He looked over at Robert. "Want a sniff?" He wadded up the rag and the can and handed it over.

"Sure, why the hell not?" Robert had about ten vials of crack stashed in his car, but that was over at a lot near the park, and he was feeling edgy. He soaked the rag and held it up to his face, trying to ignore the stains. Inhaling deeply he felt his head grow huge and pulse in an uneven tempo. He closed his eyes, watching the light trails on his eyelids, like stars at night. He was numb all over, and even the burn in his nose felt good. He could feel his heart race, and when he opened his eyes the overhead lights ebbed in rhythm with the throbbing of his head.

"Thanks." He handed the stuff back, and tried to sink into the concrete wall as the effects of the chemical left him. He sat and thought about sleeping. His lawyer sure as shit didn't seem to be in any hurry to get him out, and he didn't know anyone else to call. He closed his eyes, trying to ignore the snores of the drunk on the bench or the nervous tapping that his inhalant buddy had started against the floor.

All at once it seemed he was waking up, alert to the sounds of shouts and footsteps outside the cell. Several of the men in the room moved to the door and looked out, but jumped back when it slammed open and three cops came in, hands on the holsters of their guns. One of them looked around the room at the faces of the men and barked, "Which one is Morris?" For a split-second Robert thought he was getting out, and he started to stand up slowly, his legs asleep. He didn't move quick enough for the larger of the cops, who yanked him all the way erect with one hand while the other reached for his handcuffs.

"You Robert Morris?"

"Yeah, what the fuck is going on? Am I getting out?" Right before the nightstick slammed into the side of his head and he sagged into the arms of the other officers, he knew that, somehow, he wasn't going home.

CHAPTER 24

They left him alone in a room. Robert looked around and thought it was the same one he had been interrogated in before about the mall thing, but he couldn't be sure. These places all grew to have a certain sameness after awhile. Outside the door the place was in more of a panic than usual. The cops that had pulled him from the holding cell had seemed on edge, almost frantic. He didn't get an answer when he asked what was going on, and they wouldn't tell him if his lawyer was around.

So he sat, waiting for the detective they called Banks. He supposed it was the older guy he had seen in the park, in the car with Adam. He had already told everything he knew about the job, which wasn't much, to some guy named Maxwell. Nobody had said a word about any shootings, and Robert hoped nobody tied him into the thing with Kenny, that kid from the Masquerade. He got up and looked out the window into a hallway. Nobody there. He wanted a cigarette.

The sound of the door slamming open behind his back scared the shit out of him. So did the cop who walked in.

"Sit the hell down."

He did. The man looked tired, almost haunted. Robert thought about asking what was up, but decided that silence would be better.

"You know what's going on out there?" The detective asked, rubbing his eyes with both hands.

"No, I've been down in holding, haven't seen my lawyer or nothing. Nothing happening down there."

"Well, just to let you in on it, your buddy Adam escaped." The man pulled a pack of cigarettes out of his jacket and lit one, making a face. "Haven't smoked since I was a kid. Your pal walks out of here an hour ago, and I smoke half a pack. Now you're going to tell me everything you know about this asshole or, I swear to god, I'll hurt you in places that you didn't even know you had." He sat at the table, smoke floating up to the hooded light above his head. "I'm waiting, shithead."

"What the fuck? I'm supposed to be best buds with this guy? We just met a few weeks ago, I swear."

"How did that happen?" Nelson asked.

"He showed up at one of the clubs-Velvet I think. Said he remembered me from that day at the mall. I got pretty scared, I mean, that guy don't play, you understand?"

"No fucking kidding. So what, you guys hang out, have a few beers, go see a ballgame?" Robert could tell the man thought he was wasting his time. Guy made him nervous.

"No, dude doesn't drink. Yeah, weird ain't it?"

"Some people can do it, you know." Nelson responded. "Some even go without crack. Now tell me where the hell he would go? Where did you meet him? What was he driving?" He stood up and walked around the table until he was between Robert and the door. His size blocked the light from overhead, and for a moment all Robert could see was a jagged silhouette of a crazy person, hands clenching, standing above him.

"Listen," his voice a little shaky now, "I don't know any of that stuff. I met him the other night at the Majestic Diner, he told me to be at the park around eleven. He gave me a radio, and told me where to sit. Then you guys come along, and here I am. That's all I know."

Nelson backed across the room, and Robert was relieved. Maybe this clown will buy it. Of course, it was the truth. He didn't know where Adam would be, other than long gone. Still, this guy looked pretty shook up. Maybe he should have his lawyer in here. Couldn't hurt to ask.

"You know, I got rights! Where's my lawyer? I ain't talking until my lawyer gets here." He leaned back in his chair, crossing his arms behind his head. It left him totally vulnerable when Nelson spun and slammed the back of his hand hard against Robert's face. The force drove Robert and the chair backwards, down to the floor, where his head hit with a smack. In an instant the detective was over him, shouting, his hands at the collar of his T-shirt bouncing his head against the floor.

"You got rights! Rights? Same kind of rights that the man in the mall had? Same rights as those poor saps who were stupid enough to try and take a trip the day your boy blew up the airport?" Robert felt himself begin to black out as his head tattooed the hard floor. "Don't tell me about rights. I've been working for twenty-five years making sure dickheads like you have rights, and I'm fucking sick of it!" His face was red and swollen, a balloon about to pop. Robert tried closing his eyes, moved his arms up to try and knock Nelson's hands away. Finally the man stopped, and Robert rolled into a ball and tried to stand. His head was on fire, and he could feel blood on his neck, matted in his hair. Nelson sagged against the wall, rubbing his hands like they hurt.

"I'll get your lawyer, you piece of shit. And we'll all sit in here and you'll tell me what I want to know, you understand?"

Robert rubbed the back of his head, and slumped into a chair. He would have to say something, just to get this guy to calm the hell down.

"Sure, whatever."

As the door slammed shut Robert looked at the place on the floor where they had been. A slick spot was spread across two or three of the tiles. He felt the back of his head, and hoped that it would stop bleeding soon.

"Bastard's going down." Robert thought, his head pounding.

It was about twenty minutes before the door reopened and his lawyer and the cop came back in. Nelson looked more in control, and the two men were followed by a uniformed cop carrying a tape recorder. He set it up on the table and plugged it in.

"That'll be good. Stay around out there, in case I need something else." Nelson told the man.

"Sure thing." The door shut.

The pain in the back of Robert's head had diminished to a dull throb, and it felt like the bleeding had stopped.

"See what this asshole did to my head?" he said to his lawyer, a younger man Robert had only met once before, when he was arrested on the crack thing. He had gotten the gun charge thrown out, and pleaded out the crack holding to probation. Pretty good, considering, but the guy was expensive as shit. They all were.

"Yes, I do. That's a matter for another time. We'll get you to a doctor in a little while. Right now you need to talk to this man, or there isn't anything I can do for you, you understand?"

Robert picked at the grime under his nails for a moment before answering.

"Am I gonna get out of here, or what?"

Nelson responded. "If you tell me where this guy is, and anything else you know about him, like I asked you before, then sure, you can walk. If not, I put you back in the holding cell and let you think some more. Okay?" He turned to the lawyer. "Arliss Robinson, right?" The man nodded. "I'm Detective Nelson Banks. You mind if I tape this?"

"You didn't have that in here when you assaulted my client before, did you?" The lawyer looked smug, like lawyers are trained to look.

"Assaulted? Robert's chair slipped. Right, Robert?" Nelson was grinning.

"Fuck you. I'm having blurred vision." He felt safer with the lawyer in here, at least Nelson wouldn't start pounding on him again.

"I think that's from all that rock you smoke."

His lawyer cut him off. "That's enough. We have no objection to the tape recorder. I'm sure my client will cooperate in whatever manner he can." He took a legal pad out of a briefcase and marked the date on the first line. "What exactly happened here, and how does it involve Mr. Morris? You don't think he had anything to do with the escape, do you?"

"No, I know Robert couldn't help with Winter's leaving, seeing as how he was down in the tank. It's just that he's the only one who had any contact with this nut, and I want to know what he knows." He turned and looked at Robert. "Now tell me where you think Adam is going to go."

Robert sat for a minute. "I never found out where he was staying. He gave me a phone number, that's all."

"Let me have it." Nelson reached for the lawyer's pad of paper and prepared to write.

"555-0202, I think. It's a cell phone, so I don't know how much good it's gonna do ya."

Nelson scratched the number on the pad and tore off the page. He opened the door and handed the paper to the cop outside. "Give this to Maxwell, tell him to run it for an address."

The door shut and Nelson returned to the table. Robert hoped that the phone number was enough. He didn't have any other cards to play.

"What kind of car was he driving? You see that?"

"Only the van at the mall, remember I told you about that?"

"Yeah, we checked it out. Nothing came of it. You never saw him drive anything else, he never mentioned where he was staying?"

Arliss spoke up. "I think Robert has told you that he doesn't know anything else. Unless you have some other questions, or you want to book my client, I suggest you let us leave and attend to his head injury." The lawyer looked down at the floor, where the blood had dried to a faint pink color. He looked back at Nelson, and for a moment the two men stared at each other.

"Yeah, all right. I got more important things to do than sit around and listen to bullshit. Robert," he said to get the kid's attention. When Robert looked up at him he continued, "Robert, your lawyer is going to explain what's going on here, I imagine. I want you to understand that we will pull you back in when we need you again, right? So don't think you're walking out of here free and clear. Counsel, I trust you'll explain the situation to your client?" Robinson nodded yes and began putting his things back into the briefcase.

"I understand, detective." He stood, and motioned Robert to do the same. "I wish you luck with getting Winter back."

"Yeah, sure thing. Don't let Morris here leave the state, anything like that, you understand?" he said as he walked out of the room.

Robert had attempted to get the lawyer to tell him what was going on, but the man wouldn't until they were out of the station.

"You need a ride to your car?" Robinson asked.

"Yeah."

Robert told him where he had left it and they walked across the parking deck to the lawyer's car. Morris was enraged at the beating, and he could feel a lump under the skin at the back of his head. He wondered if the cops where going to pull him back in if they couldn't find Adam.

As the lawyer pulled out of the lot and headed down North Avenue Robert shifted in the seat, trying to hold his head away from the backrest.

"So are you going to tell me what's going down? Nice work, you getting me out of there. Thanks."

"I had nothing to do with it. They let you out so they could follow you, see if you lead them to Adam." The lawyer turned and looked at him. "I'm telling you this so that you know. Don't give these people any reason to come after you. I don't know what the story is with you and this Winter creep, and I don't want to, either.

Just don't have anything to do with him, and don't screw around and get picked up, or Nelson is going to come down on you like a ton of bricks."

"Like he already did?" Robert rubbed the back of his head. "What are we going to do about this? My head still hurts, you know." As they drove Robert watched as they passed the Masquerade club. Place looked like a dump in the daylight. He wondered if Kenny was around, if he had any supply he could unload. The ten vials in his car wouldn't last long. He had been counting on Adam giving him some cash after they left the park, but that had gone to shit. He needed money, and he wanted a gun. He never had trusted cops, and if what his lawyer said was true, and he imagined it was, then he needed to have some insurance on his side, just in case he got hassled. He didn't want to end up in some dark parking lot at midnight with a bunch of pissed-off cops using him for a soccer ball as they had Rodney King.

"We are going to lay low. You're lucky they didn't press charges on you. If they catch this guy then you probably walk. If they don't in the next few days then they are going to haul your ass back in and book you. Now isn't the time for you to start any shit, you follow me?" Arliss turned the car down Piedmont, nearing the parking lot where Robert had left his car.

"So what you're saying is that I got lucky when I got the shit beat out of me?" Robert was getting madder all the time.

"Basically, yes. Is this the place?"

Robert could see his car parked up near a dumpster. Didn't look like anyone had messed with it.

"Yeah. Pull up near the black Camaro over there." As soon as the car stopped his hand was on the door, ready to get out. Robinson put his hand on the boy's arm, holding him.

"You can't have any contact with Winter, you understand? If he calls you, wants you to help him out, blow him off and go to the cops."

"Are you serious? If I go the cops then I'm sure to get fucked with. You think I'd cross that Adam guy? He gets the idea I talked, he takes me out before I get a word out of my mouth."

"Well, whatever. Just lay low until this gets cleared up. You still at the same address, in case I need to get in touch with you?"

"Sure, same place." He didn't want to have any more to do with this guy. He was only a step or two better than the cops, Robert felt. He had paid this guy a bunch of money already for a retainer, so he didn't expect to hear from him again. He told him so.

"I have to work with these people, Morris. It makes my life a lot easier if I don't piss them off. If they ask me to bring you in for more questions, then I need to be able to find you. If you don't like that, find another lawyer."

"You'll give me my money back if I do?"

"Not a chance."

CHAPTER 25

Adam knew that if he listened long enough, waited patiently, he would see a break. So he had remained still on the bench, his two handlers staring off and on at him, and waited. Finally, after about five hours someone came by to tell him he was being moved in preparation for the arraignment in the morning. The two cops had taken him from the cell, both looking a little wary, and wishing that they hadn't been relieved of their guns when they entered the squad room, per procedures.

Gradually a ragtag line formed around the doorway to the stairwell. A sign above read "Basement" and Adam expected that they would be transported from there to another part of the building, or maybe to the courthouse. He was shoved into the midst of ten or so other men, all handcuffed and looking around. Some anxious first-timers, others bored, veterans of the process. It was a situation of hurry up and wait. Adam watched as forms were checked, papers initialed, keys found and doors unlocked. One of the men assigned to him left his side to make a call and his partner was busy jawing with another cop, looking back at his prisoner from time to time. Adam turned slightly, and saw the other cop captured on the phone, trying to explain his way out of a missed date.

"I have to take him to central, he's gonna be arraigned at nine Monday." The man held the phone away from his ear as the phone squawked.

"It's my job, Carla, that's why. Think of the money I'll get from the overtime ... what? No, baby I can't right now, I told you what I have to do." The man nodded as he listened.

"Listen, I've gotta go. Maybe one day, you get a job, you see what I mean. See you later." He hung up the phone and moved to his partner's side, looking at Adam as he walked by. He waited while the other man finished relating a story that he had already heard twice. He turned as he felt a tap on the shoulder.

"What time you guys going to come back?" The man said, glancing at a clipboard.

"Hell if I know. All I know, as soon as we make the drop-off, I'm done for the night." He kept looking at the cop in front of him, standing with a jacket over his hands, as if he was on his way out, and he couldn't put a name to the face. Of course, in a precinct as large as this, you never learned all the faces, and he rarely worked this late, so maybe he had missed a few people. Guy didn't know him either, or he would have used his name.

"Yeah, they got you guys babysitting some piece of shit? I guess they took him over by himself." Over his shoulder Ramon could see the line moving ahead, through the open door into the stairs that led to the parking lots.

"Stop the line, hold up!" He shouted, his stomach suddenly turning sour. Panicked, he did a quick head count, and where before there had been thirteen, now there were twelve. Son of a bitch. He turned to tell the cop to hold up, they might need some help, but the man was gone. Son of a bitch.

Hide in plain sight. In a roomful of cops, the easiest path was to look like one. He did, and walked down the steps out of the squad room. He knew that no one would recognize him if they saw him for the first time, but he kept an eye out for Banks. He knew the man had watched him in the car when they brought him in, studying his face, learning it.

He was near enough to the doors leading out that he could hear the traffic on Confederate Avenue. He walked at a normal pace, hands in front of him, draped by the jacket he had lifted off the back of chair. It covered the handcuffs which would be all right for a little while, but he still had to get rid of them.

Walking up the sidewalk, his eyes scanned the people he passed. The walkway was only slightly crowded, being a Saturday. On a workday it would be teeming with those brave souls who worked in downtown Atlanta, but on a weekend the homeless were in the majority. A block away from the police station was an abandoned space, and he could see a group of men standing around at the corner of the lot, talking to each other or just staring out at the world. He moved along the perimeter of the area, eyes on the ground. Soon he found what he needed, the screw-off cap from a bottle of wine. He knelt and picked it up, continuing to walk until he reached the back edge of the lot, where it ran up against a building. He crouched down, and made sure that he was away from the sight of those on the street and sidewalks. The men in the opposite corner glanced his way, but made no effort to investigate any further. It was the law of the streets - let it be.

He had to strain his hands to tear the metal apart, trying to separate a strip of the cap from the rest. He succeeded in getting the metal to start to come apart, but couldn't get his hands close enough together to finish it off. He grabbed the sliver of metal in his teeth and pulled with his hands. The metal resisted, and then came apart and flew out of his mouth, cutting his lip in the process. He tasted blood but ignored it, and picked up the strip of metal. It was stiff enough, but looking down at the lock on the cuffs he knew it was too wide. He put it back into his mouth, avoiding the cut on his lip. It took longer than he expected, but after about five minutes he was able to fold the metal over itself, and it looked the right size.

The effort had worn him out, but he knew he didn't have time to rest. Angling the pick down he got it into the lock, and steadying his free hand against his leg, he twisted the metal around until he felt the catch release and heard the click that said freedom. He quickly did the other side and tossed the cuffs into the high weeds of the field. He left the jacket behind him on the ground as he walked off, rubbing his wrists and sucking blood off his lip. He could see three police cars in the streets, moving slowly from block to block, hunting for him.

He had money and a change of clothes in the car, but it was far away and probably impounded by the cops, since he had been forced to leave it in a grocery store parking lot when he went to meet Erin. He didn't know of any way they could tie it to him, because he had rented it on a stolen credit card and didn't leave anything in it.

He thought about his options. He had to leave the city, and do it quickly. It hadn't been luck alone that had enabled Banks to catch him in the park, without knowing what he looked like. The man had figured out Adam's secrets, some of them anyway. He didn't want to give the man a second chance.

He had to change his clothes, because the police would be on the lookout for a man in gray pants and a dark shirt. The problem was that it was Saturday, and the only places open downtown were fast-food stands and movie theaters. He felt in his pockets-empty. The police had taken his money and wallet when he had been booked. He felt a kinship to the homeless people he passed on the street, adrift in a world of affluence without the entry fee. But unlike them, he had skills that would provide escape from the streets. He had only to use them.

CHAPTER 26

Nelson and Maxwell sat at adjoining tables in the break room, having a drink and some chips, the only food they would see for the rest of the night. Banks felt responsible for Winter's escape, it was his man. He ran over the facts again in his head. Philip stayed silent, taking some shelter from the storm that raged above them, as units were dispatched to find the escapee, damage control. He knew Nelson would talk when ready, so he waited.

"You got somebody following Morris?" Nelson asked, smoothing the bag from the chips in front of him, a nervous gesture.

"Two plainclothes are in place, and a car at his house if he ever shows. You think he's gonna run?"

"Not if he's smart. Right now he's more valuable to us here, and he should know that. Or at least his lawyer should have made it clear. I imagine he wants Adam picked up as much as we do."

Philip cocked an eye at his partner. "Why's that?"

"I don't think our boy likes to leave loose ends. And right now he's got two wandering around that we know of, the Morris kid and Erin Welch." Nelson shook his head as he thought of Erin. He dreaded telling her of Adams's break, but he knew he had to. If he was right, and he felt he had a good enough understanding of the man's mind by now to think he was, then Erin was in danger.

"You get her yet?"

"No, nobody answered the phone. I guess I'll swing by there later, do it face to face. Shit." He crumpled the bag in disgust and tossed it into a garbage can.

"You want me to send a car over, have them do it?"

"Nah, I got her into this mess, I should be a stand-up guy and see to it myself."

"Nelson, it wasn't you on that phone that night, remember? Remember what that poor sap in the hospital looked like? Erin caused that to happen, not you. All you did was give her a chance to make it right, or at least better. You did what any of us would have done, given the odds we're up against with this guy."

Nelson smiled, barely, at the notion of odds. "Yeah, I think our odds went off the freaking board when that motherfucker waltzed out of here."

"We'll get him," Maxwell replied confidently, sounding surer than he felt.

"Twice? No damn way. I mean, sure, we could luck up and grab him, but with any sort of head start this guy's gone, adios." He stopped for a moment and thought back to the park, walking Adam up the path with the sun pouring down and the end of a nightmare almost in sight. Thinking back, if he had been able to have his gun, just for that brief moment, then this would be over.

"Bang bang." Banks blew imagined smoke away from the end of his finger. Philip looked up, surprised.

"What?"

"Nothing. Just some wishful thinking. Let's go get this asshole."

CHAPTER 27

Erin walked around her house as though she was a zombie, the darkness outside deepened by the haze of scotch she wrapped herself in. He had looked right at her. When their eyes locked, impossible she knew through the glass, but she had felt it anyway, she had heard a voice in her head. It was laughter. She told herself it was her own, but she couldn't be sure. She hadn't heard the words of the detective as he had walked her to her car, and she had no idea how long she had sat in the house without turning on a light, just sipping whiskey and watching, but not comprehending the television.

Ralph had been by during the day, a quick note on the refrigerator saying he was going back to the office, and don't wait up. Don't worry, she thought. I won't. Thanks for the Chivas though, she laughed, pouring another drink. She felt so tired, as if she had run for miles and miles in the hot sun, and it brought a sense of numbness that made the sounds from the TV seem so far away. The more she drank the harder it became to focus on the images that flickered on the screen. Maybe she should take a shower, try and get just a little bit sober. But the shower was upstairs, further than she felt like moving at the moment. Anyway she liked feeling a little drunk, or at least she liked feeling little at all.

The picture on the TV changed, showing the logo for the upcoming news at six. Erin sat up a bit on the couch, trying to see what was going on. The pictures looked familiar, somewhere she had seen before, but she couldn't place it. Why was the person on the screen not talking? She looked closer, blinking her eyes to try and clear them. She rooted around on the couch until she found the remote control and pressed the mute button. She must have hit it when she had reached for the bottle the last time. In the silent room the brassy voice of the newscaster seemed louder then it should, or perhaps she thought it was the words the woman was saying. As the blonde spoke, Erin recognized the scene over the woman's shoulder. It was the front of the police station on North Avenue, where she had been that afternoon. She hardly noticed her glass fall to the carpet as she listened to the words.

"To recap our top story tonight a prisoner has escaped from the Atlanta Police Services building. The man, Adam Winter, was being held on murder charges stemming from the knifing of an Atlanta contractor at Perimeter Mall earlier this month. Police sources tell us that the handcuffed man simply walked out of the station a little over two hours ago and vanished onto the streets of downtown Atlanta. Police are warning us tonight that the man is considered armed and extremely dangerous, and they have provided us with a copy of Winter's booking photo."

Erin stared as his picture filled the screen. It seemed to hang there, and the eyes looked the same as they had that afternoon in the lineup, boring into her head. The face was replaced by a shot of a press conference. Erin turned the set off, and the room was plunged into darkness.

Tears came, first slightly, but then grew into sobs. I can't stop shaking, she thought. She jumped up and looked out the window, seeing nothing in the light of the streetlamps outside. She ran to the back windows, and slammed her hand into the wall, trying to turn the lights on. She felt pain as a nail popped off in the attempt, but she ignored it as she looked out at the large yard, dotted with clumps of pine and dogwood trees. On any other day they filled her with happiness, the things she had planted. Now they looked like hiding places, still and dark, perfect for a person to kneel behind and watch. And wait. She backed away from the window, slowly letting the curtain fall back into place, hoping that the motion wouldn't be seen from outside.

Why? He knows that I'm in here, my car is in the driveway. Slowly she felt along the wall until she came to the stairs leading up to the second floor. She scrambled up, locking herself in the bedroom. She waited a few moments for her eyes to adjust to the dark, and when her breathing slowed enough that she didn't feel like she was on the verge of blacking out, she reached across the bed and picked the phone up off of the table. She realized that she didn't know whom to call. Kathy would be no help in something like this, and if she called 911 and there turned out to be nothing going on then she would feel foolish. Try the detective first, and then call 911. She felt in her shirt pocket until she found the card he had given her that afternoon. She could barely make out the numbers, but gradually she did. It rang far longer than she imagined a phone at a police station should ring.

"Hello, Detective Banks' desk."

"Yes, I need to speak to Nelson Banks please." Erin tried to keep her voice steady.

"I'm sorry, lady, but he's out in the field right now. Is there something I can help you with? Or would you like to leave a message?"

Erin replied no, and hung up the phone. She punched in 911 and quickly, thankfully, a voice answered.

"911. Can I have your name please, and where you are calling from?" The voice sounded bored, and every few seconds a beep came over the line.

Erin started to speak when she heard a car door slam. She dropped the phone, and dove off the bed. In the stillness of the house she couldn't hear anything, but she knew that didn't mean much. She peered slowly out the bedroom window, keeping her head below the level of the sill as much as she could. Around the bend that her house sat on she could see a small, dark car. It was stopped, but not parked. She could see that the running lights were on, but she didn't see anyone near the car. She rose up a little further, and tried to see down onto her yard. The shadows from the trees all looked like silhouettes of men, stretching long across the grass. Near her head she could hear a buzzing from the phone. She reached over and tried to put the phone back, but it slipped off. The noise sounded like thunder in the room. She looked outside again. The car was gone.

She got up slowly and walked across the room. She felt like a sitting duck. Had that been him? If it wasn't now, it would be soon, and here she sat, alone, without a chance. She wanted a drink, but the bottle was downstairs. At least up here she had a chance to be aware of someone coming in downstairs. Like that would do her any good, she thought. I need something to protect myself with.

Her eyes shot across the room, to the closet. She opened the door and felt past the coats until she found Ralph's shotgun. He always said he was an outdoorsman, but she couldn't remember him doing anything with the rifle other than cleaning it. He had tried to show her how it worked, but she had blown him off, saying that she didn't want anything to do with guns. She remembered enough, however, to check if it was loaded. It was. She sat down on the edge of the bed, feeling the heavy, cold weight of the gun on her lap. She would wait until Ralph got home, and he would be able to help her, to protect her. Even as she finished thinking that, she knew it was a lie. He hadn't protected her before, and in fact had told her to give up. She looked at the phone, and contemplated calling 911 again. But she had tried the police, and they hadn't been able to protect her either. The only person who had protected her was her, and look what that had gotten her. Sitting in the dark in fear of every sound, ready to spend the rest of her life looking over her shoulder to see if her mistakes had come home to roost. No, she had been the only one that could do it. As she brought the barrels up to her lips she remembered the phone call, and the picture she had seen in the police station.

Who can protect me from me?

CHAPTER 28

Nelson dreaded meeting with Erin. He wanted to protect her, and had assigned a car to patrol the neighborhood, but he knew that nothing short of catching Adam before he got to the house would make her feel safe. A person's first instinct in a situation like this where you had to impart bad news was to soften the blow, dance around the subject in general terms and hope the message got through. That wasn't his style, and in this case no amount of candy coating would make it better. She knew what Winter could do, and if she had half a brain she knew that chances were good that he would come looking for her.

He pulled into the driveway of her house, looking up at the windows. All were dark, and the house leaked a strange feel, as if it was closed up and dead. He parked behind Erin's car, and as he walked by he laid his hand on the hood. It was cold. She had been here awhile. Maybe she turned in early but glancing at his watch he saw that it was only eight in the evening. It seemed like years ago that he had been in the park, thinking that his nightmare was almost over, instead of beginning in earnest.

He knocked on the door, rang the bell. He could hear the chime sounding in the silence. No one answered. He looked around the street from where he stood on the front step. Maybe she is asleep, give her a few minutes. The rest of the neighborhood looked quiet, well cared for. He could see bikes lying across one yard, a baseball bat tossed into the garage of another. The sight of the bat made him remember why he was here, and he knocked again, louder. Still no answer.

He headed around the side of the house. Maybe she sits outside in the evening, like he use to, before this all got so crazy. He rounded the edge of the house and pulled up quick, his hand instinctively going to his gun. The back door was open, just a touch. He watched it for a moment, and a breeze blew it back into the house, and then it slowly closed again, never shutting. Something was wrong.

He looked across the back yard. No one seemed to be in the grove of trees, and he couldn't tell if anyone had been there recently. Releasing the strap on his holster he knelt down, and crept slowly up to a kitchen window. He moved up, and looked at the room. All he could see out of place was an ice tray on a counter, dripping water onto the floor. He walked under the window, came up to the door. The sounds of the night became dimmer as he focused his attention on the house. He couldn't hear anything. He pushed the door with the knuckles of his left hand, his mind already treating the area like a crime scene. He tensed as it opened into the house, waiting for a reaction. None came. He took his gun out and moved into the room, shutting the door behind him with his elbow. He listened intently, but heard no sound.

"Erin?" He called out, loudly in case she was asleep, although he had a bad feeling she wasn't. He couldn't be sure, but he thought he smelled cordite in the air, the scent that comes from a gun being fired. He called again and got no answer. He waited a moment, poised, to see if his entrance flushed anyone out. He waited until his instinct told him he was alone in the house, and then he started to walk.

Cautiously, he moved past a dining room table, and entered the den. An open bottle of scotch sat on an end table, a glass on the carpet in front of a couch. His stomach tightened even further. He walked over to the couch and looked quickly around, scanning for blood, signs of a struggle. Other than the glass, it looked normal. The door to a bathroom stood open across the room. It was empty. He led into the room with his gun, eyes focused. He stared at his face in the mirror. He was sweating, and wondered if he should go outside and call for backup. Too late now, he figured as he backed out of the bathroom and headed toward the front of the house. He looked out the curtained windows beside the front door. He watched the street, quiet as before. Behind him was a stairwell, and looking up he knew that the smell of a gun was stronger now. He could almost see it hang in the air.

He walked up the stairs, one at a time, pausing every few steps to listen. The house was still. He reached the landing at the top and looked around. Four doors. One was open, and he could see into the bedroom beyond. He went in. Papers and a small laptop computer covered a desk, but other than that the room seemed empty. He checked the closet, smelling the tang of mothballs.

The next door was a linen closet, filled with carefully folded sheets and towels. The next door led into another bathroom, this one empty as well. He stepped into the hall again and listened as a car passed the house, radio blaring. He could hear the laughter of a young girl rise above the music, and then it faded. He waited until it was quiet again.

He walked to the last door, the only one shut in the entire house. He tried the knob but it wouldn't give. Locked. He called for Erin again, hoping against hope that he would get an answer. The only sound he could hear was the beeping of a phone off the hook. He slammed his shoulder into the door, cursing the pain as the door gave and slammed open.

The smell of gunpowder filled his head as his eyes came to rest on the bed, his stomach rolling. Fuck. She had pulled a Hemingway, or these days a Cobain, he guessed. Out of habit he knelt beside the body and felt for a pulse on the neck, but as soon as his fingers brushed the cooling flesh he knew it was pointless. Beyond the bed he found the phone and depressed a button. When the dial tone returned he punched in the number of dispatch and called the shooting in, telling the girl to be sure and send a morgue van.

He knew that he would have to go over the area inch by inch in the next few hours, but he wouldn't start it now, not until a team showed up. He couldn't stay in the room anymore. He went back downstairs, into the den. He sat on the couch and closed his eyes. He knew that they would eventually rule that Erin had killed herself, and he also knew just as strongly that it really was just another Winter killing. Just as sure as if he had fired both barrels into her head, the fear of him had killed her. The bottle of scotch on the table looked good, but he knew better than to use the glass on the floor. He didn't want to explain his fingerprints. He reached into his coat pocket and drew out a handkerchief, grasping the bottle by the neck. He drank, and it burned as it went down, but he felt the warm numbness travel out from his chest. Good. Enough of this and he could almost forget what lay upstairs.

As he started to put the bottle back down he saw a blinking red light on her answering machine. He reached over and pressed the play button, his fingers still covered by the cloth. The machine rewound and he waited for it to play. When the voice came on he stood up in a rush, rage filling his soul like black ice.

"Hello, Nelson. Recognize me?" Nelson resisted the impulse to scream. "I trust you have been upstairs. Before you start cursing my name, I didn't do it." Fuck yes you did, he thought. "She was already gone when I got here. As for you, we won't be meeting again. I don't do cops, if I can help it. Too much heat." Nelson grinned, sickly. You don't know heat yet, my friend. "I'll be long gone by the time you listen to this, so this is good-bye. I just wanted to offer you a bit of advice." Nelson felt his stomach tighten, in fear, revulsion. "I'm leaving this way of life, going home. You had a chance, a chance to end it, but instead you trusted the system that raised you. Now so will I. You won't be able to find me, no one ever has, but if you ever come close, I tell you this." The voice paused, and Banks thought the machine had quit. It started again, lower, menacing. "You will be my last."

CHAPTER 29

Robert drove aimlessly, just to kill time. The inside of the Camaro was dark, and he turned down the dash lights leaving only a faint glow. As he rode over the railroad tracks that crossed Montreal Road the beer bottles on the floor rolled together, annoying him. He pulled into a parking lot lit by only a few lights in a far corner. Rolling down the window he felt the sticky heat of the Georgia night cover his face. He reached down to the floorboard and gathered the bottles, flinging them out the window. The area was silent, an office park during the week, now just a hangout for local teens to drink in. The exploding bottles sounded like gunshots as they struck the concrete. He reached onto the seat beside him and gathered another bottle, this one larger, more potent. He uncapped the top and drank, feeling the vodka ice his throat.

It had been about five or six hours since Arliss had left him at his car, and Robert was bored, bored and angry. He couldn't make a move, not with the cops watching him. He had already smoked about half the crack he had stashed in the car, and he was afraid to get in touch with anyone for more. He looked out the windows. No one passed by, and he didn't figure anyone would. He had grown up here and gone to high school just down the road at Tucker. Or at least started to, but never finished the tenth grade. One suspension too many and he had left, leaving his parents' house and the safety of suburbia for the reality of the city. He remembered nights like this. Hot, quiet, and endless they seemed when he was younger, smoking dope with the other stoners. He never saw many of them after he left. It was like he had dropped off the face of the earth when he moved downtown, into the crash pad apartment that some chick named Kimba had turned him on to. He grew and experienced more in the first six months there than he had in his previous sixteen years. Kimba had been a dancer until her attention was diverted solely into drugs, buying and selling. She had used Robert as a mule, sending him into the night with bags of dope and rolls of bills. He had looked so young then that most people just thought he was some kid out on the town. He made twenty bucks every time he made a run for her, and he felt that he had the whole thing licked. Making good money, free dope, and an endless train of women to enjoy. All of this had ended the night he came back and found Kimba stretched out on the floor, a hypo in her arm and a thin trail of blood leaking down her chin.

This first time he had seen death it scared him, almost enough to go home. Instead he cleaned the apartment of anything of value and moved on, not even calling 911. It wasn't his deal. After that he felt like he had graduated, moved up to a new level. No more being a bagman, instead he fell in with some guys with common interests, and over the years he had hung with them joyriding, smoking crack, making a buck here or there. Some of them had been busted, others died, some like Kimba, others like Kenny's girl. He had been lucky so far.

But now, he was pissed. It was just a matter of time before the cops hauled him back in and demand he lead them to Adam. Like he could. He had never learned where the guy lived, and in fact couldn't really tell you much about him at all. Robert had been afraid of Winter the first time Adam had come to him and told him he knew who he was. Now, however, he was pissed at him too. Getting involved with him had been a stupid thing to do, he knew. Guy like that draws too much heat, heat Robert didn't need. What Robert needed to do was split, get out of town. He had friends down in Jacksonville; maybe he could head down there.

First he would need supplies and cash. He had a roll stashed back at his house. Load up and leave, before the cops started getting nervous and pulled him back in. He drained the bottle and tossed it out the window to join the others. He reached under the seat and brushed aside the pistol while reaching for the plastic bag. After filling the pipe he inhaled, letting the smoke drift out the window. Just a buzz to get motivated. The crack sizzled in the bowl, turning black as it heated. Robert closed his eyes and saw clouds, moving slow. He ran a hand through them, feeling the softness on his fingers. One more hit and the pipe was empty, the vial finished. He tossed it out the window and reached onto the floor of the car for a CD. Sliding it into the player he started the car and pulled away. The flat, hard voice of Ice-T filled the night as Robert lit a cigarette. He drove slowly across the lot, looking for cars. He hadn't seen a cop yet, but he knew they were out there, waiting for him. He swung the car out onto the road, turning up the music. Ice-T and Body Count, jammin' on *Cop Killer*. It wasn't rap, he couldn't stand that shit. This was okay, more like metal. Anyway the song was cool, about dusting cops. Robert knew one that needed it, that old fuck at the station. His hand went to the back of his head, felt the knot under the skin.

> *"I'm a cop killer check it out and see*
> *I'm a motherfuckin' cop killer*
> *Better him than me"*

The guitars raged and drums slammed. Robert turned it up more, until the dash rattled with the sound. He was out of booze. Up the road was a package store. He would hit it and then head for home, grab what he needed, and book.

It was dark on the road, so when the headlights of a car came up behind him he saw them at once. He drove on, about fifty feet ahead of the car. He slowed to a stop at a light, blinking red in the night. The car behind him pulled up and suddenly the inside of the Camaro was filled with pulsing blue lights. Shit.

An electronic voice came from the unmarked police car. "Stay in the car. Keep your hands on the wheel." Robert reached onto the seat beside him and picked up the crack pipe and the baggy. His eyes stayed on the car in the rearview mirror. It looked like one cop, as far as he could tell. He moved the stuff under the seat, and grabbed the gun. The tape played on, the force of the music merging in his head with the flash of the lights from the car behind him. He watched in the side mirror as the man got out of the car, and started to walk up to the Camaro. He put his hands on the steering wheel, and waited.

"You mind turning that music down, son?" the cop said as he neared the window. Robert could see that the guy didn't even have his gun unhooked. From the side he could see movement in the mirror and he looked back. There had been another person in the car, another cop. He was out of the car now, checking Robert's tag. He felt the gun under his leg. He hadn't expected to be picked up this soon.

"I said, turn that shit off, now." Robert took his hand off the wheel like he was going to reach for the CD player. Instead he grabbed the gearshift, popping the car in reverse. He could see the eyes of the cop behind the car get big as the reverse lights went on.

"Fuck you, asshole." Robert said as he brought the gun up, firing into the man's face and hitting the gas at the same time. Both men went down, one with the side of his head blown into the bushes at the edge of the road, the other with a crushed pelvis. Robert dropped the car into neutral, kicked open the door. The cop on the ground was twitching, his hand reaching into the folds of his coat for his gun. His face was white, what was left of it. Robert fired again, into the chest. He lay still after that. Morris turned at the sounds of the man in back trying to breathe, his chest crushed. Robert fired again and the man's head snapped back and then slumped onto the trunk of the Camaro. From inside the car the CD went silent for a moment between songs, and Robert listened for sounds in the night. He could hear the cars down the road at the intersection, and the crackle of the radio in the unmarked car. He moved to the side of the white sedan and yanked open the door. As he leaned in and turned off the radio he saw the video camera mounted on the dash, a red light blinking. Robert swung the pistol at it, knocking it off onto the seat. He picked it up and found the eject button, discharging a tape. In the distance he could hear the whine of a siren and he dropped the tape to the ground, crushed it with the heel of his boot. Satisfied that it was ruined he flung it into the high weeds that lined the road.

He got back in his car and looked at his face in the mirror. A spray of red drops misted his forehead, and he wiped them off as he put the car in gear, moving up the road. He could see the bodies of the men in his mirror, motionless in the glow of the blue lights. The music played on, like a soundtrack.

CHAPTER 30

Nelson moved through the scene at Erin's house, answering the questions put to him in a sort of daze. The personalizing of the case by the tape made him wary, nervous.

"Didn't Morris give you a number for Winter, said it was a cell phone or something?" Maxwell asked him as they stood in the front yard, watching the paramedics take the body away.

"Yeah, we checked it out. No record of it. Why?" Banks returned, his mind elsewhere.

"Well, let's go inside, listen to the tape again. I think it was made on the run."

The men went back into the house and Philip motioned Nelson toward the machine. It was coated in fingerprint dust like most surfaces in the house. So far the only prints seemed to have come from Erin and Nelson. Most likely, Banks thought, Adam had worn gloves. Maxwell reset the answering machine as Nelson watched. They listened as the tape played.

He had listened to the message enough times for the initial shock to wear away, leaving only anger. As the voice spoke on, Philip stopped the tape.

"Hear the way it faded out somewhat, then came back?"

Nelson answered. "Yeah, so what?"

"That means most likely he made the call from a car, and he was getting out of range for a second and then came back. You follow me?"

"No, not particularly," Nelson said, ready to move on.

"The way these cellular phones work is that the signal from the phone is relayed to a transmitting tower, like a radio wave. There are dozens in the metro area, and they provide pretty blanket coverage. It's just that when you go from the edge of one area to the edge of another, the signal isn't as strong. So you get the fade like we heard on the tape."

"Okay. How does that help us?"

"Well, it means that for at least a little while, Winter was using a cell, and wasn't in one central place. Which isn't really good news, since it means he is on the move."

"Great, just great." Nelson sighed.

"Could be good ... I mean, if he's still using the same phone that Robert gave us the number on, then we have a shot at tracking it, like they did with Simpson out in L.A."

Like most overly technical things Maxwell tried to explain to Nelson, this too went past his area of understanding. Still, he trusted the man, and was desperate for any sort of lead.

"Move on it. Do what you have to do. I'm getting out of here for awhile."

"You gonna be where I can find you?" Philip asked.

"Sure, just need to get a few things. I'll check in later."

CHAPTER 31

Adam stared down Peachtree Street, feeling the crowds move, his body a shadow in the doorway of an abandoned building, one of dozens in the area. He could break in, lie low for a while, until the heat died down. But he was tired-tired of hiding, of working, of staying safe. He wanted to leave, to go home and wait for the end to come. He had no idea when that would be, but he hoped it came sooner instead of later. He did know one thing, assuredly. It wouldn't come on the streets of Atlanta.

He kept watching the people as they went from place to place, killing time from shops to fast food dives. He picked a store that looked crowded and entered behind a crowd of Latinos, invisible to the clerk's eyes. He made his way to the back of the store, and moving quickly, grabbed a shirt and some pants off a rack and took it all into a dressing room. He clawed off the clothes he had been arrested in, tossing them on the floor. Pulling on the new ones he could tell they were cheap, but it didn't matter. He wasn't planning on wearing them long. He finished and looked up over the stalls. A video camera was mounted on the ceiling, in plain sight. Looking at it he laughed, seeing that there was no cord leading away from the back of the unit. In a store this small the owners relied on the illusion of security, unable to afford the real thing, hoping that no one would notice the difference. It was attitudes like those that had allowed Adam to prosper.

He left the store, not even getting a glance from the clerk, engrossed on the phone, her back to the store. As he opened the door to leave a chime sounded. The clerk never moved. Hide in plain sight.

Leaving the store the heat of the day seemed to wrap him tightly, like a wet shirt. He walked until he found a parking deck, ducked in. He cruised down an aisle, his head up, looking down a line of cars, just like everyone else who can't remember where they left a car an hour before. He was hunting for something plain, one that no one would notice. He spotted a tan Ford near the end of a row, away from the steps and in deep shadow. He walked past the hood of the car and slammed his hand down. No alarm sounded, but he hadn't expected one. Going around to the side he looked in. Messy as hell. The front doors were locked, and he sighed, annoyed at having to pick the lock to get in until he noticed that one of the back doors wasn't locked. A box of crayons lay strewn across the seat. Some kid went off and didn't lock the door. Thanks. He got in and bent under the dash, pulling wires free. He had the car started in fewer than sixty seconds and drove out the main entrance past a cop in a patrol car at the edge of the street. Their eyes met, but Adam knew the man didn't see him, at least not the face he was looking for.

As he made his way into the traffic he flicked the radio on, tuning the sad sounding unit until he found some classical music. The elegance and power of it filled him with peace. He stared down the road, watching the intersecting streets grow less frequent until he felt the heat of the city leave him.

He was going home.

CHAPTER 32

Nelson drove, letting his mind clear, going from place to place with no real pattern, on autopilot. He had passed by the park, not thinking of seeing Adam, just touching base with all the sites, immersing himself in the case. He knew that just letting his mind go where it wanted, without restraint, had in the past turned up new ideas. Maybe it would again.

He had been past the mall, crowded with weekend shoppers, traffic snarled. It was here that it all started. Ground zero, at least as far as he was concerned. He knew that other bodies, other lives lay ruined and unclaimed elsewhere, but they had nothing to do with him, not today. If he found Adam, locked him down tight, it would all be over and then they could work it back, get answers to other questions. If he found him.

He, not they. The police hadn't lost Winter, he had. It was his name on the tape in Erin's house, and it was now a hunt between two men. Adam had been right on the tape. He had trusted the system, and got beat at it. Maybe the time for believing in the process had passed. Nelson knew the metro area police were on alert, searching. But they would never find him, even if they looked straight into his eyes. Nelson was the only one with even a ghost of a chance. He chuckled at ghost, because that's what he was frigging chasing. Smoke, masks, a phantom.

The sun was going down behind the trees. Years ago, nightfall on a Saturday night meant more work for a cop, more calls, more action. People worked all week and then the weekend rolled around and they let off steam. Come Sunday morning it would calm back down, and life would go on as before. Now it was seven days a week, twenty-four hours a day. No one did anything different come the weekend, because they didn't do anything the previous days. He wondered where Robert was, if he was thinking of making a run, out of sight. If he was smart with a sense of self-preservation he would, because Adam was sure to come for him.

Nelson checked his location, and drove until he came to the entrance ramp for the interstate, merging into the traffic. Construction vehicles dotted the side of the road, with cranes towering over the work sites like silent birds of prey. The roads in Atlanta were forever under construction or expanding with the promise of completion before the Olympics. Right. Until people stopped moving farther and farther away from the city to live the roads would never be big enough. And he didn't imagine that anyone would be moving back to town anytime soon, back into the jungle.

He left the highway and traveled in the direction of Robert's house, past the stadium. The closer he got to downtown he noticed the cars getting a little older, a little louder. Things had to last longer down here, if they lasted at all. He saw houses set on the side of the road, paint peeling and weeds standing high, but usually with a new Jeep in the driveway, or maybe an older Caddy, tricked out with a cheap paint job. People living on the edge, government checks the only source of income, life a constant balancing act between needs. Some slipped and fell, ending up on the streets, forming the invisible layer of human waste that dotted the landscape of the city. Abandoned, their houses went unclaimed until the crack dealers moved in and started a smoke house, the only improvements being heavy steel doors and a supply of runners, clockers with beepers and guns, ten years old. It was in this environment that Robert lived, his means and way of life not much different from the others who had lived here for generations, although you probably couldn't tell him that.

His phone sounded and Nelson picked it up. He'd never get the hang of this damn thing. His idea of heaven was becoming a place where no phones rang.

"Go ahead."

"Nelson, it's Philip." The voice sounded excited, eager to talk.

"What's up?" Banks asked.

"We got a trace on the cell phone. Close enough, anyway."

It took Nelson a minute to remember what Maxwell was talking about.

"Oh yeah, the number we got from Morris? I would have thought it was ditched by now."

"Nope. It's still going. We've tracked it across the city, but it seems to be sitting in one place right now."

"Where's that?" Nelson wondered aloud.

"First you got to understand, we can't pinpoint an exact location with this thing, only what we call a 'range', about three miles."

"Shit, that could be anywhere," Nelson responded in disgust. Three miles would cover a lot of downtown Atlanta and surrounding areas, and he had figured that much out himself. "So where are we talking?"

"Somewhere near the stadium. Most likely near I-20, around that area."

Nelson looked up. He was on Dekalb Avenue, running parallel to the Marta tracks that formed the artery from downtown to the suburbs. His house was near Glenwood, only a few miles from the general area Philip had named. He sat quiet for a few minutes before speaking.

"What's the address on the Morris kid? It's somewhere around there, right?"

"Let me see." Nelson could hear Maxwell moving papers around, cursing at his disorganization. "Got it. 379 Monument Avenue. You anywhere near there?"

"About three blocks. We got somebody down there, watching the place, right?"

"Yeah, but he hasn't showed, at least not that we have seen. We can't get close without looking really out of place."

Nelson laughed picturing the sight of two plainclothes cops sitting in a car in a neighborhood like that. They would be made for cops in about thirty seconds, like the days he used to work the projects and was greeted with shouts of "5-0 in the house!" every time they would walk into one of the tomb-like apartment buildings. The only thing they would do would be to spook off Morris if he showed, keep him on the move.

"Any chance of getting some guys into the house across the street, next door or something?"

Maxwell snorted. "Are you fucking kidding? After dark these people don't even answer the door for their own families. Not a chance. They just sit inside and pray for daylight."

"Yeah, I know what you mean. Thanks." He switched off the phone and put it back in its holder. Praying for daylight. He'd been doing the same thing for years.

CHAPTER 33

The classical music had ended hours before, replaced by something called "The sounds of America". He didn't seem to hear it until a version of *Basin Street Blues* came on, played by the Dirty Dozen Brass Band from New Orleans. Adam had heard this song hundreds of times played in the streets of his home. It made him eager to leave, to put the miles behind him. He wanted to cross over the big bridge and lose himself. He felt dull, soft. He needed to be on alert, now more than ever. Just get out of the city, onto the highways, where he could blend into a pack of travelers and be just another face in the crowd. He would have to get another car, ditch this one before it showed up on a hot sheet. He couldn't take the chance of some overeager traffic cop pulling him in, not now. If he was ever to fall back into the hands of the law then Nelson would have him, and he wouldn't have the chance he had before. He had seen a look in the detective's eyes that said he would have rather shot him down than submit him to the legal process, a game that either side could lose. Adam knew the detective wouldn't do that again.

One last stop before he could leave, one last loose end that needed snipping. He had been too late at Erin's, his work already done. He knew that it would end that way, not surprised at all. When people come face to face with a chance to beat their demons, they might win the battle, but in doing so lose the war. Stripped of all the rationalizations and excuses that people use to hide their innermost desires, they find nowhere to hide, no turning back. Once Erin had made the connection in her soul between the man on the floor of the mall and her boss, her demon, she couldn't step back. And once she stepped forward, she died. It was just a matter of time before her mind told her body.

So only Robert remained. This one, this one he hated to do. He had seen so much of himself in the boy, which is to say he saw nothing. No soul, no heart, a slate wiped clean of fear and remorse. Only a flame of self-preservation, looking for the next reason. Any reason. He would have to be careful, cautious. Robert had the instincts of a city rat, able to hide, blend in, coming up for air only to feed.

Adam drove down Moreland Avenue until he reached the parking lots that marked the beginning of what was known as Little Five Points, a mecca for both the hip and the hopeless of the city. Teens with rings in their noses brushed shoulders with homeless men carrying brown bags with wine inside, each claiming the turf for his own. Adam could move through here unnoticed. He pulled the car into the lot, past the orange cones that marked the pay-to-park zone. The car would sit until at least next week, until some storeowner noticed it for a second time and called the tow company. By then he would be long gone. He wiped the car down, removing his fingerprints and reached under the seat, checking the fanny pack to make sure he had the gun. He thought about tossing the phone in a dumpster, but that would be stupid. If it got found it might lead back to him, somehow. He'd ditch it in a lake somewhere, let the elements take their course. He exited the car and started walking, heading away from the Saturday night crowds, down Moreland. From the doors of clubs he heard music, loud, angry atonal sounds that hurt his ears. Robert listened to that trash, had tried to play it around him once. It had set Adam's teeth on edge, and he picked up his pace to get away from it. It was now fully dark, and as he left Little Five Points it got quieter, the only sounds those of cars passing, or the rumble of busses as they went back and forth. Ahead a few blocks he could see a group of guys standing on a corner, in front of an empty store, a For Rent sign hand-lettered in the window, yellow with age. They glanced at him as he passed, sizing him up, wondering if they should make a try for the bag around his waist. Adam's eyes found the face of the biggest one, a black guy well over six feet tall, his head shaved clean, and with arms the size of most people's legs, roped with veins. He held the man's stare until he was abreast of him, and waited until the other man dropped his glare. Adam didn't think the man would try it. Stare down the big dog, and the other ones wouldn't matter. They parted and let him by, silent. He walked on, dark houses on both sides of the road, the only things lit being liquor stores. In a few minutes he had reached the top of a hill, overlooking I-20. Robert lived less than a mile from here. He kept walking, alert to the types of cars going past now. No sign of a black Camaro, but that didn't mean anything. Robert most likely would be holed up at home, waiting for the police to find Adam and take the heat off of him.

Turning down past a sign reading "Welcome to East Atlanta" the sounds of the street dimmed. No one stood on corners here, the houses quiet. It was if the entire area had gone to sleep, or was deserted. Few streetlights shone, only about one in three. The city couldn't pay the tab to have the bulbs replaced, so they sat there useless, abandoned.

He passed a road called Patterson, and stopped. He was one street away from Monument where Morris lived. At the end of the street rose a cannon barrel, atop a little grassy knoll at the intersection. The armament was from the Civil War, marking the death of a southern general in battle. Adam wondered if the people who lived here, almost all of them black, had any feeling about the memorial. It made him wonder if these people noticed anything at all past themselves.

He started to walk down Patterson but stopped at the sight of an nondescript sedan parked on the road. In the darkness of the area it looked empty until the red glow of a cigarette flashed in the window. Plain clothes cops, he knew. He altered his route, moving past the street. Any white man walking down here would be enough to raise the suspicion of the pair in the car, interest he didn't need. He looked at the houses along his sides, and cut between two that looked empty, no lights on, no cars in the driveways, careful not to rouse any dogs that might be out. He found a grove of bushes at the back of one of the lots, tangled with honeysuckle. He knelt in the darkness, the sweet smell of the plant filling his head and waited.

CHAPTER 34

Robert watched the houses around him grow dark, lights shutting off, the only sign of life at all being the jumping blue glow of a television from a window. He didn't think the cops he had offed had taken the time to run his plates before they approached the car, but he couldn't be certain. He was sure his lawyer was right, that they would be watching him anyway, to lead them to Adam which was the last thing he wanted to do. So he stayed in the darkness of the night, surrounded by the shadows of a car, long since left to rust on the side of a vacant lot. His legs were getting tired from crouching, and he really wanted to smoke some more rock, but all that was in his house and he didn't want to chance it. He had ditched his car further down the street, in the back of a supermarket that had been empty for weeks. He would have to take his chances that the packs of kids that roamed this area wouldn't boost it to go joyriding, but he didn't want to be found in it. He had the feeling that it would be better if he just waited and watched the area for a while, at least till sunup. His eyes had adjusted to the darkness like a cat's, and he could see past the houses across the street, onto Patterson. He had seen the undercover cops come up and stop, and had watched another cruise past the front of his house three times in the last few hours. After awhile they would stop, he imagined. Right now they didn't really concern him. He was more wary of Adam, and he felt sure that he would come on foot, as silent as a panther. All of his lawyer's talk about loose ends had made him nervous. He was ready, ready to take the fucker out if he showed.

Another car crept down the street, like the others before, but instead of going on past this one stopped, the engine cutting off. The silence was almost as loud as the motor had been, and when door shut and Nelson got out the slamming sounded like a gunshot. Robert watched the man walk up to his front door, and shine a flashlight in the windows. He peered into the dark house for a little while and then walked around the side, to the back.

Robert cursed, not needing this right now. He crept from the safety of the car and moved across the street, losing himself in some overgrown hedges that rimmed the edge of his next-door neighbor's house. He watched the older man snag his shirt on the rose bush on the side of the house, and he knew what the thorns must feel like, surprising him in the darkness. Not as much as the next surprise he would get, Robert thought, rising up in the night.

Nelson knew that this was a dead end, that Morris wasn't going to show, but he had to check it out just the same. The house was a piece of shit, about forty years old and in need of repair. The yard was overgrown, but he wasn't surprised, not able to see Robert as the type to be out weeding. As he neared the back of the house his arm caught something and he jumped, pulling it back. He shined his flashlight on a large wild rosebush that covered nearly the entire side of the building, including a window. Sure as hell beats burglar bars, he thought, his arm stinging from where the thorns had taken hold. He felt nervous, edgy. The whole area was quiet, dark and silent. In his neighborhood a person prowling around at night with a flashlight peering into windows would have people on the phone to 911 in a minute. Not here. These weren't that sort of folks, and even if they did call there was no guarantee that a patrol car would show up in time.

He went around the side of the house, and saw a little deck, overcome with bushes, a planter box in the middle of it. Out of the middle rose an untended Japanese red maple at least five feet high. The idea of such beauty existing in a shithole place like this made him stop. He wished he were at home, with the time to enjoy things like this. When this was all over he would. It would be time to pack it in, get out before the same things that had killed his father found him and turned him inside out, left him for dead. He could feel them around him now, and if he didn't finish this thing off, like he should have before, they would take him.

Adam could sit for hours, motionless, watching. He felt secure trapped in the bushes, and would just wait to make his move. There was no sign of life at Robert's house, but he knew that he would be here soon, if only to get more drugs. Adam couldn't imagine walking around feeling like that, but it seemed that everyone he met dosed themselves with something. From scotch to crack, it was all the same. He never wanted his senses dulled, so he had avoided it. Maybe Robert would return here, and just sit around and get high, which was most likely the only way he had to pass the time. Then Adam could get him, when he was less aware of his surroundings.

The area around him flared with light as a car pulled up in front of Morris' house. It was Banks, the cop who almost had him. This was a bonus, although not unexpected. Nelson was from the old school, duty bound. His losing Adam would be a black mark, one he could never forget. He had hoped just to leave the area, far away from Banks, leaving only a cold trail across the country. He didn't want to kill the cop, not wanting the heat that followed, but now the man was just too close, and it would be too easy. He watched him some more, waited as he looked into the dark house and found it empty. He went around the side out of Adam's line of sight. Adam reached for the zipper of the bag at his waist and reached in, pulling out the gun. Walking across the street, a shadow in the dark, he clicked off the safety.

Robert stood at the back of the grass in his own yard or what had been grass years ago; before Robert had rented the place and let it go to shit. Like he cared. The man who owned the place was afraid to even come down here anymore, and the tools he had given to Robert lay rusting in a small shed at the side of the lot. Robert moved over to it and looked in, searching for something heavy to use as a weapon. He couldn't risk the sound of the gun, even though gunshots around here weren't that uncommon. He didn't want to bring the plainclothes cops around, not yet. He picked up a short sledgehammer, left here for Robert to use when he needed to cut up some firewood. Like he had time for that shit, he laughed. Still, it would be mighty handy as a club, feeling the heft of it in his hands. The metal head was rusted and would reflect no light, not that there was any around. He returned his attention to the man on the deck. He seemed to just be sitting on the bench, looking up at that ugly red tree that grew in the little box. Just like his landlord. He got all bent about it too, going on about the "grace of nature." Give me a fucking break, Morris thought as he crept down the side of the fence surrounding his lot, nearing the man, motionless in the dark.

Nelson shook himself, unaware of how long he had remained on the wooden bench, staring at the tree. He was tired, past the point of simple rest. His mind felt blank, spent. It took him a few minutes to remember why he was here, but then he did, and he felt even more exhausted than before. He felt sheltered here, away from the phones, and radios, the world. Staring at the tree he felt like he was in a beautiful place, peaceful. Still, regardless of what he thought, there was a world out there, and he had a job to do. He rose, ready to go. He needed to call Maxwell, see what was up. He supposed he should have brought the phone with him, but he never remembered it until he was somewhere it wasn't, and needed it. He stepped away from the bench, moving a branch of the delicate maple tree to the side, out of his way. He was staring at a face, a shadow in the dark. It made him stop, momentarily freezing him, while he tried to figure out who or what it could be. When the vision spoke, he knew in a instant who it was, remembering the voice from the interrogation room, snotty and defiant. An instant too long, too late.

"Wrong place at the wrong time, dickhead. See how you like having your skull smacked around, like you did me." Robert said as he brought the hammer down, into the man's head. The figure crumbled to the deck, and Robert waited, waited to see if it moved. It never did. He listened as the flashlight rolled out of the man's hand and off the edge of the deck, and then the night was silent. It remained quiet, still. Robert could hear nothing except the dim sounds of traffic from the streets far away. He flipped Nelson's jacket aside and grabbed his gun, stuffing it in the waistband of his black jeans. He walked away, ready to get to the car and take his chances. He didn't have the means to get rid of the body, and didn't want to be here when the patrol cruised by again and noticed the unmarked car out front. He moved off the deck into the yard and slipped past the house, looking up at the silhouette of it, certain now that he could never return. He walked as silently as he could past the old woman's house beside his, not wanting to wake the dogs she kept in the yard, her "security system" she would laugh and call them. Not much good if they are all old and asleep, like they always were. He made it past without disturbing them, watching the ears of the fattest one twitch in its sleep. Wonder why they do that, he pondered. As he got to the front of the house he stopped, looking out at the street. No cars went by, and it was dark. He started to move, but held up when he heard the sound of feet in the gravel alongside his driveway. He waited to hear it again, but nothing came. He returned to the back of the house, looking up at his deck. Whoever it was wasn't a cop, because they didn't have a flashlight out. Whoever was up there wanted to remain hidden. Robert had a good idea who it was.

Adam came up the driveway to Morris' house, careful to avoid the rosebush along the side. In doing so he walked into a gravel area next to the driveway, and the sound of his feet on the stones echoed into the night. Damn, he said to himself, moving as quickly as possible to the back of the house. Have to pay more attention to what's going on, at least until he got out of here, finished up. He was glad that the light above the back door was dark, and the area seemed deserted. He knew the cop had come back here and hadn't left. The deck was caged in by privet bushes, blocking sightlines from the surrounding houses. He stepped onto the deck and stopped, his foot starting to slide in something slick. He looked down and followed the trail of blood that started in a pool under Bank's head. Son of a bitch, Adam thought, as he felt the cold steel of a gun barrel on his neck. His hand moved slowly to the bag on his waist, and he knew that the running was over, that he was as close to home as he would ever get.

He handed the pistol carefully over his shoulder, butt end first. The image of a runner passing a baton to the next came up in his mind, and in a way that was true.

"Use this one. It's quieter."

EPILOGUE

It was getting dark again, and the scenery rushed by in a blur, one town after another the same. The driver didn't see it, his eyes locked on a point that seemed just ahead, but that was never reached. The radio was silent, his head pounding. He didn't know where he would stop or what he would do when he did. Something would come up. Something always did. He felt stiff, and knew he should get out of the car, walk around and stretch himself out, stay loose. It was raining as it usually did around here. He could see why the old man had left it years before. He turned down a road that ran alongside a river, the water reflecting a heavy moon, not seeming to move at all. He saw a sign ahead, slowed to read it. Green River National Park. He pulled into a parking lot. It was deserted, and the only lights were those in the little hut across the pavement that housed the bathrooms. That reminded him of another reason he had to stop. He turned off the car, listening to the rush of the river near him, calling to him somehow. He opened the door and got out, leaning against the side of the old car, watching the river flow. Inside the car a phone rang and he cursed, and thought about ignoring it. He was tired and needed a rest. Instead he reached in and picked it up, remembering where he had come across it, long ago.

He answered as he always did, in a flat, emotionless voice that gave no clue to its source.

"Hello?" The man waited. Sometimes he would get back only silence. Sometimes not.

"Is this Adam?" The woman's voice sounded hesitant, unsure.

"No." He didn't feel like offering any information until he got a handle on who he was talking to.

"Well, I spoke to Adam before at this number, is he around? I need to speak to him."

"He's not available."

"Well, it's just that I need him for something. He did some work for me before, well, I guess it's been awhile now, and I need to hire him again." The man waited, to see if she would go on.

"Adam's not working anymore. Maybe I can help you." This was how they all used to come, for awhile until his name got known.

"You in the same line of work? I had him dispose of something before, and I need it done again. Think you can help me?"

"Sure. Just don't talk about it over the phone. I'll meet you somewhere." He thought a moment and then named a busy mall about five miles away. She described herself and asked how she would know him, what did he look like.

He smiled and just laughed, hanging up the phone. Hide in plain sight.

To do what thou wilt shall be the whole of the law.

Aleister Crowley
The Book of the Law, 1904

The survival of the human species is by no means an
obvious thing.

Noam Chomsky, 2009

Authors note:

This book was written in 1995, shortly before the summer Olympic games in Atlanta. As John Lennon once said: "Life is what happens to you when you're busy making other plans." And such is the story of why this is just now being published, in 2009. Obviously at the time of writing the book the tragedy of 9/11 had not occurred. When I revisited the work in order to publish, I decided at that time to not update the book to include it, because it would have only served to amplify the basic tenet of the book, not change it.

James Mann, 2009

www.ingramcontent.com/pod-product-compliance
Lightning Source LLC
Chambersburg PA
CBHW020127180626
46810CB00004B/1437